Time Tantrums

Ginger Simpson

ISBN-13: 978-1495943775

ISBN-10: 1495943771

Electronic edition of **Time Tantrums** published by:

Books We Love Ltd.
Chestermere, Alberta
Canada

ASIN: B007TOS7BO

PROLOGUE

Mariah
Colorado Territory—1872

Mariah Cassidy sat on the front porch and watched her husband, Frank, ride through the gate. The large Rocking C, the ranch's emblem, cast a shadow across his face as he rode beneath it. His muscled thighs gripped the flanks of his huffing, black stallion, and his hat rested in that familiar rakish tilt. He certainly knew how to sit a horse.

Frank dismounted and gave the horse's reins to a hired hand. He dusted himself off then turned and strode to the porch. "Good morning, sleepyhead."

She smiled. "You were up bright and early. Would you like some breakfast?"

"No thanks. I already ate with the ranch hands, but... I might be interested in somethin' else."

Even after seventeen years of marriage, Frank's innuendo embarrassed Mariah. Just a wink of one of his heavy-lashed, blue eyes made her heart flutter, but her desire for lovemaking never equaled his. She fretted about him leaving her to find satisfaction in the arms of another. Her mother had planted such deep-seeded inhibitions within Mariah that nudity made her uncomfortable. She loved being in his arms, but beyond that, her embarrassment got in the way of feeling free.

The same old thoughts niggled at her as she gazed into his face. Why didn't she feel the same comfort with her body as Frank did with his? *Would* he be happier with someone else? He deserved a wife with passion to match his own. She massaged the creases in her brow.

"Mariah, did you hear me? Would you like to join me upstairs?" He nodded toward the house.

She held up a silencing finger while guilt niggled her. "Hush. The children will hear you."

* * * *

Taylor
Denver, Colorado—2002

Lost in thought, Taylor Morgan sat and stared at the stacks of files piled on her large mahogany desk. The sun barely peeked through the office window of the high-rise building and the dim lighting matched her somber mood. Had she remembered to kiss David before she left home? It seemed she was always in a hurry these days. Rushing to put on make-up, darting off without goodbyes, working late, and barely finding time for her husband—something had to change. She didn't want a repeat of the argument she'd had with David last night.

The thud of his fist on the dining room table echoed in her head. When he expressed frustration, her body trembled, much the same as the silverware had. She'd never seen him so angry.

His words had cut through her like a knife. "We're like ships passing in the night. All we do is work, eat and sleep. You're so busy with your job that that's all you think about. You don't cook, you don't clean... Good God, we only make love on your schedule, never mine. What if I don't want to wait five years to have children?"

The thought of having a child made Taylor shudder. She'd labored hard to achieve the status she enjoyed at the law firm. Giving up *now* wasn't an option. Still, what about David? Didn't he have a right to the family he wanted? She felt so conflicted. What if her husband wasn't willing to hang around until she determined the time felt right?

If only there was a way to compromise. She nodded. Making David a priority seemed a good start if she wanted to save her marriage. Tonight, she'd leave work early, go home, and make dinner. A few candles, a bottle of wine—David would be pleasantly surprised.

She picked the most pressing files from her desk and threw them into her briefcase, planning to peruse them while she cooked. Grabbing her jacket from the chair, she slung it over her shoulder and reached the door when the urgent buzzing of her intercom summoned her back. She leaned over the desk and mashed a button with her fingertips. "Yes?"

"Ms. Morgan," her secretary responded, "Mr. Abernathy requests that you join him in the conference room right away. The senior partners have called an emergency meeting."

"I'll be right there." Taylor plopped her briefcase back on the desk. She straightened her collar and smoothed her skirt then took a deep breath.

Maybe tomorrow, David, maybe tomorrow.

CHAPTER ONE

Colorado Territory—1872

Mariah Cassidy awoke to whinnying horses outside her bedroom window. She rolled over, propped herself on an elbow and pushed the lace curtain aside. Despite the morning sun's blinding glare, she saw Frank, and several ranch hands moving animals from the corral toward the west pasture. The clock in the parlor downstairs chimed seven times.

Her mouth gaped. Surely, it wasn't that late already. Why hadn't Frank roused her? Normally she had breakfast over, the dishes washed and put away. She threw aside the colorful patchwork quilt and scooted off the bed. Where were the children?

After pulling her sage green gingham dress over her head, she smoothed it down over her petticoat and stepped into her shoes. She poured water from a pitcher on the washstand into a matching white porcelain bowl and dipped a cloth into the cool liquid. Leaning closer to the wall mirror, she inspected her face. Oh, those dratted lines and wrinkles!

It bothered her to be thirty-five—especially being wed to the most handsome man in Colorado. But aging was inevitable, so she hurriedly finished washing then pulled her long auburn hair back and twisted it into a bun. In the privacy of their bedroom, Frank loved seeing her hair down, but for housework and all the other chores around the ranch, it wasn't practical or acceptable. She tucked a wayward strand behind her ear then hurried off to the kitchen to start breakfast.

The Rocking C kept everyone in the family busy. Callie helped with the washing, cooking and cleaning, and Jacob fed the chickens, cleaned the barn and did whatever else his father determined. Whatever time left in the day was devoted to studying at home. The closest school was hours away.

Mariah walked by her fifteen-year-old daughter's room, surprised to see Callie still sleeping. Was Jacob up? Why in the world had Frank left them in bed? He usually maintained strict rules about the children getting their chores done in a timely manner. Puzzled by his behavior, Mariah stuck her head in the doorway. "Callie dear, time to get up. We have things to do."

With the same red hair, green eyes and fair complexion, she reminded Mariah of herself when she was younger. The marked difference: a spattering of freckles across her daughter's nose and cheeks, and Callie hated them. Jacob had twice as many, but they looked cute on a ten-year-old boy.

Her daughter rolled over and squinted, her eyelids heavy from sleep. Pushing her quilt away, she stretched her arms over her head. "Be right down, Ma." Her words slurred in a yawn. "Soon as I get dressed and comb my hair."

Mariah went into Jacob's room. The usual mess littered the floor: clothes strewn about, boots left where he walked out of them, and the odor of a youngsters sweat and dirt lingered in the air. She crossed to the bed and ruffled his curly red hair. "Jacob... Jacob, wake up. Pa expects you to get your chores done. We're going into town today. Remember?"

Jacob swatted her hand away. "Ah Ma, can't a fella get any rest around here? As soon as I smell breakfast cookin', I'll get up. 'Sides, I got plenty of time to get my chores done."

Mariah left him still snuggling beneath his quilt and

looking angelic. She chuckled as she went downstairs to the kitchen. "Can't a fella get any rest?" Where did he come up with such things?

She pulled a heavy cast iron skillet from the oven and plopped it atop the stove—a surprise gift from Frank. He'd ordered it from the mercantile catalog then drove the wagon two days to pick it up and bring it back in time for their anniversary. She enjoyed being married to such a thoughtful man, and thankful she didn't have to cook on the hearth anymore. Of course she wasn't the only one to reap the benefits; her family did, too.

The bacon turned crisp and brown, and eggs sizzled sunny side up in hot grease. Mariah cupped her mouth. "Callie, Jacob, come down. Breakfast is almost ready." She pulled biscuits from the oven.

Her daughter stumbled into the kitchen, still half-asleep. She stifled a yawn while she held out her plate for Mariah to fill. "Smells good, Ma. Sorry I slept in this morning. I stayed up late reading my history primer."

Mariah smiled. "You're excused. At least you have a good reason for being sleepy. I like that you're eager to learn."

Jacob was another story. Getting him to study was like milking a stubborn cow. Nothing but predictable, he'd race down the stairs at any moment, following his nose. As anticipated, he entered the kitchen like a whirlwind. Unruly curls hung past his eyes, and his shirt gaped from improper buttoning. He snatched up a plate and stood behind his sister, peering around her. "Don't eat all the bacon, Callie." He gave her a shove.

"Jacob! There's plenty to go around. No need to act like a heathen." Mariah stifled a grin, wiped her hands on her apron, and knelt in front of him. "When are you going to learn to fasten your shirt the right way?" Her fingers worked to redo his buttons. "And stop fidgeting!"

"But, Ma…."

Before he protested his starvation, she rose, filled his plate and set it on the table. "Sit and eat!"

Deciding to skip breakfast, she settled for a cup of coffee from the pot Frank had left simmering at the back of the stove. She filled a mug with the aromatic brew and sat down with the children.

"Callie honey, when you're through eating, get the kitchen cleaned up, and Jacob, before you go outside, *please* clean your room. It's worse than the pigsty outside."

"Smells like one, too," Callie interjected.

Mariah raised her brow. "Never you mind Callie, just eat and keep your comments to yourself."

Jacob stuck his tongue out at his sister.

"All right, you two." Mariah rolled her eyes. "That's enough. As I was saying, Jacob, after you're done with your room, get the chickens fed before your pa takes a switch to your backside. And don't dawdle! We're already getting a late start on our trip to town."

Mariah left the children eating and went upstairs to her room. While she straightened the bedcovers and fluffed the pillows, she pondered the three-hour trip by wagon. Although a long, bumpy ride, the trek offered the children uninterrupted time with their father. It seemed the ranch occupied him most days.

While making a mental list of things to pick up at the mercantile, thoughts of the upcoming May Mixer drifted to mind. Every spring, all the families from the surrounding areas gathered to celebrate the end of winter, and she needed material for a new dress and perhaps some matching ribbon.

Callie had mentioned looking forward to seeing the handsome, new mercantile clerk who'd caught her fancy on the last trip. He definitely was a good-looking young man, but Mariah worried that at fifteen, her daughter seemed far too young to be interested in boys.

Mariah peered at her reflection in the mirror. "Have you forgotten that you were only a year older when you promised to marry Frank?"

She grimaced, wondering how her daughter had grown up so quickly. Girls her age married every day. Her own courtship came to mind. It seemed ages ago that Frank had proposed. Her feelings for him hadn't dimmed despite the passage of time. If anything, she loved him more.

She pinched her cheeks to add some color, then dipped her fingers into the washbowl and dampened a wisp of hair that refused to stay in her bun. The natural curl she inherited from her mother wasn't her favorite attribute, but then neither were the occasional gray strands she promptly plucked. With a final check of her appearance, she picked up the porcelain bowl and gingerly carried it downstairs.

Mariah emptied the used water, set the container aside and began preparing sandwiches for the trip. When she finished and stashed them in a basket, she poured a second cup of coffee and stepped outside to steal a relaxing moment on the porch. Frank had built the stylish overhang to cover the entire front of the house, making this her favorite place to spend time. Standing at the honeysuckle-trimmed railing, she inhaled the wonderful aroma swept up by the mild May breeze. The gentle northern wind transported the ranch's earthy smells and rippled the sea of green grass beyond the barn.

Looking out over their vast acreage warmed her. She and Frank had worked hard to build their legacy, and she counted marrying him was as one of life's biggest blessings. She'd grown up never feeling connected to any place for very long, and having roots was wonderful. Her father, always a dreamer, had dragged his family from town-to-town, always searching for something better. Mariah met Frank at a church social, and after a short courting period, they married. He was a hometown boy with no desire to travel, and for the first time in her life, she knew security.

"Hey sleepyhead." Frank interrupted her thoughts. Somehow, he'd crept up without her notice, even while leading his horse.

Her cheeks warmed. "I feel guilty getting up so late."

"I decided to give everyone a break and let ya'll sleep later than usual. I ate with the boys in the bunkhouse. It wasn't as good as your cookin', but it was fillin'. I wanted to get some the horses moved before we left."

She smiled. That was her husband, always working. Together, they'd built the Rocking C—a two-story home with a whitewashed barn and corral fences—on land Frank had inherited from his father. A large herd of Longhorn cattle grazed the open range with the several head of horses they also owned. She took a last sip of coffee, smiling at the thought that someday everything would belong to their children and grandchildren.

Frank leaned into her line of vision. "Where are you? Seems like your mind's a hundred miles away."

"Sorry. I was day-dreaming." She placed her cup on the railing and massaged the small of her back. "I fed the children, and there's some bacon left over. Can I get you something? Coffee?"

"Nah, I'm fine food wise… but I might be interested in something else." He winked a heavy-lashed lid at her.

She gave a dismissing wave. "Oh, Frank, hush. The children will hear you."

He grinned and scuffed his boot in the dirt, but when he looked up, his blue eyes showed a hint of sadness. "Well, if you aren't gonna take me up on my offer then we might as well get ready and go to town. I'll stable my horse and hitch up the wagon."

"While you do that, I'll round up the children and the basket of sandwiches I made this morning."

Before going back inside, she watched him saunter toward the barn, leading his stallion. Her Frank… tall, tanned with an incredible mane of dark hair always fighting against the confines of his cowboy hat. His normally short, curly hair, overdue for a haircut, now framed the nape of his muscular neck. For some reason, she always found him more attractive that way. A smile curved her lips, recalling their previous night's passion. How she loved the security of those massive arms that had grown solid from hard labor.

Her gaze assessed his well-defined upper body. Strong shoulders tapered down to a slim waistline… and those firm buttocks encased in tight blue jeans—her stomach fluttered recalling him naked. If only she felt as free with nudity as he did.

She turned her thoughts back to their upcoming trip, praying that how she felt now wasn't the way Callie reacted to seeing the young clerk at the mercantile.

* * * *

Frank pulled the buckboard up to the porch and reined in the horses. He jumped down and helped Mariah up to her seat while Jacob and Callie clambered aboard. In one agile move, Frank was back in the wagon, snapping leather to stir the horses. The rig lurched forward and, immediately, the children started picking at one another.

Mariah turned. "Listen to me!" Sternness edged her voice. "We've a long way to go and I don't want to hear bickering all the way."

"Sorry, Ma," came the chorus from the rear, but out of the corner of her eye, she saw Jacob stick his tongue out at his sister for the second time that day. Mariah chuckled to herself. What a little hellion she had on her hands. She leaned back to enjoy the silence she knew wouldn't last.

The warm, refreshing air caressed her face, but she tied a bow snugly under her chin and gave thanks for the bonnet that protected her delicate skin from the sun's harsh rays. Cuddling up to her husband, she snaked her arm through his and leaned on his shoulder. "Frank, sweetheart," she cooed. "I need some material for a new dress. You know… for the May Mixer."

He tossed his head back and laughed, then turned to her, still grinning but his brow raised . "You've got to be joshin'. You have a dress for every day of the week."

He had never denied her anything, always said that one look into her big green eyes turned him soft. Frank patted her knee. "Oh, what the heck. If you want to sew up something new and fancy, you go right ahead. Buy some material."

Looking over his shoulder, he said, "What about you, Callie? You have any plans for spendin' my money?"

"Well, Pa, it would be nice to get a new pair of shoes. I'm about to outgrow the ones I have." Callie probably crossed her fingers for telling a fib. She wanted an opportunity to talk to the young man at the mercantile.

"Well then, I guess we'd better hurry and get there so

you girls can get to shoppin'." Frank laughed again and cracked the reins against the team's hindquarters. "Jacob and I will tend to buyin' the things we need for the ranch."

For a few moments, the only sounds came from the rapid clip-clop of the horses' hooves and the rumble of the wheels against the hardened earth. The children appeared occupied, watching the tall prairie grass alongside the trail and laughing when an occasional jackrabbit darted from its hiding place. Frank stared quietly ahead.

The once fresh air smelled faintly of moisture, and the air grew remarkably still. Although only wispy clouds appeared in the crystal blue sky, something caused the hair on Mariah's arms to stand erect. She rubbed her skin to soothe the strange sensation and wondered why no one else mentioned the subtle change in weather. A cluster of wild flowers in a myriad of colors caught her attention and she pushed her uneasy thoughts to the back of her mind.

The well-traveled road held deep furrows. Frank maneuvered the wagon around the biggest ruts and bumps, but at the fast pace the ride became much more jarring. Mariah shifted in her seat, wishing for a cushion.

"Pa, can we stop please? I need to pee real bad." Jacob's voice held an urgent tone.

Frank reined the horses next to a boulder. "Here ya go, son, this should give you some privacy.

Jacob scurried behind the large rock and reappeared, moments later, fastening his pants and smiling. "Thanks, Pa, I feel better now."

When Jacob was back in his seat, Frank flicked the reins. "Giddyap," he yelled.

The horses failed to respond. Instead, they whinnied, snorted and reared back on their hind legs. One animal turned its face, displaying eyes wide with fear. The distinct rattle of more than one snake came from nearby, and Mariah instinctively knew Jacob had disturbed their nest.

"Rattlesnakes!" Frank had heard it, too. "Hold on, everyone." He leaned back and yanked the reins. "C'mon, girls, calm down. Whoa... whoa."

The wagon rolled backwards and jostled from side to side on the uneven ground. The frightened animals bolted into a dead run through deep grass and thistles off the beaten path. Mariah grasped the side and bottom of the seat so tightly that splinters pierced her fingers. Concerned with the safety of her children, she sucked her bottom lip between her teeth and glanced over her shoulder. Callie and Jacob clung to each other, their eyes saucer-like.

"Hold on, children. Hold on!" Mariah repeated her husband's warning.

Frank struggled to stop the frightened animals, but no matter how hard he pulled the reins, the horses wouldn't slow. "Hold on tight," he yelled. "The ground gets really rocky here." No sooner had Frank made the statement than the wheels hit a stony ledge, and the wagon pitched upward, before tipping and sending Mariah careening through the air like a rag doll. Her panicked heartbeat sounded in her head until everything fell silent.

Badly shaken but uninjured, Frank stood and looked around for his family. Callie, looking dazed and dirty, yet fine, sat next to a still-spinning wheel.. Jacob rose from the other side of the wagon, strands of grass dangling from his unruly locks. He brushed himself off and glanced around.

"Is everyone all right?" Frank almost released a sigh of relief, but he didn't see his wife. His breath hitched in his throat.

"Mariah... Mariah? Where are you?"

He scanned the area, wide eyes searching for her. "Mariah, Mariah. Answer me please!" His panicked tone reflected in the faces of his children.

He waited. Silence. His stomach felt as if a giant fist clamped around it.

Suddenly, an intense rumbling sound shook the prairie stillness. From an almost cloudless sky, thunder cast down a single bolt of lightning, striking the ground with energy enough to propel dirt through the air and set fire to a small patch of grass. Immediately, calm prevailed; only a single column of smoke, billowing skyward, remained as evidence.

The strange occurrence gave him pause, but fueled by the need to find his wife, Frank hurried in the direction of the fading smoke. "Mariah, Mariah, please answer me." His boots cut a path through the heavy brush.

In the far grass, beyond the wagon, he rushed toward the visible brim of her yellow bonnet and found Mariah in an oddly contorted position. Her head rested against a large rock, and rivulets of red oozed from beneath her head-covering. Frank's throat constricted. "Oh my God, are you all right? Mariah, answer me, please." His words were little more than a whisper over his choking fear.

He gently removed her bonnet and inspected the crimson-stained gash on her temple. His heart quickened. "Callie," he yelled, "Get the tablecloth from the picnic basket. I have to stop this bleeding. Quickly, Jacob, bring me the water jug."

After cleaning Mariah's wound, Frank wrapped a makeshift bandage around her head, but she remained unconscious. Why didn't she wake up? He brushed away the tear trickling down his cheek and choked back his fear. His sobbing children needed to see his strength.

Frank continued to bathe his wife's face with cool water. "Mariah, please darlin'…" He looked to the sky. "Lord this can't be happening."

CHAPTER TWO

Denver, Colorado—2002

Fifteen minutes earlier, Taylor Morgan had left her serene suburban neighborhood to drive to work. The closer she got to the city, the more congested the roadways became. Her temper flared at the usual snail-like pace of the morning commute. At a stoplight, she drummed her fingers on the steering wheel, and watched raindrops pelt the windshield. "Damn red lights." Patience had never been one of her virtues.

Today, she'd be the representing attorney in a big corporation's acquisition merger, and as usual, she got a late start. Normally her firm didn't monitor her comings and goings, but this meeting couldn't start without her. That added to her stress. Fennster & Smith's corporate executives would certainly take notice of her tardiness, and that didn't bode well for her reputation. Somehow, her good intentions to be punctual never seemed to work.

Taylor's thoughts ran back over the morning. After spending far too long in the bathroom, making sure her highlighted brown hair was perfectly coifed and her eyes properly adorned with just the right amount of liner and mascara, she'd dashed from the house, gulping down her coffee. Had she'd even spoken to her husband before leaving?

Since graduating from law school and acquiring her new position, she and David had little time for each other. He was an architect for a large firm in Denver, and their schedules always seemed to conflict. Thank goodness he had agreed to forgo having children, at least for the next five years or so. She wasn't sure she wanted any at all. Being the center of attention worked in her favor. David was a great husband both in and out of bed, and she was happy with things the way they were.

"Shit, I'm really going to be late if this damn light doesn't change." She pinched the bridge of her nose.

Her habit of cursing always annoyed David. No matter how much she tried to clean up her mouth, she failed. Too many male co-workers with crass vocabularies in her life.

The light turned green. She stomped on the gas pedal and her Lexus lunged forward. Rapid acceleration on wet pavement caused the tires to squeal in protest. Taylor glanced at the clock on the dash and wondered why she always had difficulty being punctual. If David had told her once, he'd told her a hundred times, "It's rude to be late."

Turning down a side street, and confident she'd found a faster route, Taylor darted in and out of traffic. Thoughts of her presentation spun in her head. Her heart raced. Working for one of the largest and most prestigious law firms in Denver excited her. She earned a great salary, but the demands were often nerve wracking. A glance at the clock again showed twenty after eight. She grimaced. "Shit! No more running late. This is it!"

How many times had she made that promise?

Taylor shrugged the tenseness from her shoulders while listening to the soft, jazzy song on the radio. A taxi pulled out in front of her, and she swerved into the left lane, barely missing the other car's fender. As she passed the cab, she held up her middle finger. "You friggin' idiot!" she yelled at the driver. "Get the hell off the road!" So much for tact and diplomacy, she thought, but friggin' wasn't really a word, and Hell was in the Bible….

Static interrupted her music selection. Was a thunderstorm brewing? She scrunched down and peered higher through the windshield.

Damn it! She wasn't dressed for a change in the weather. Dark, gray clouds obscured the once clear sky and the rain grew heavier. A single bolt of lightning pierced the atmosphere, sending a shiver up her spine. Fear of electrical storms stemmed from her childhood and she never outgrew it.

Already jittery from caffeine, she reached down and fiddled with the dial. Over the crackling static came the chilling sound of screeching tires, but before she spied the source, the air bag exploded in her face.

* * * *

David sat beside Taylor's bed, his heart aching at seeing his beautiful wife swathed in bandages, an IV in her arm, a tube down her throat. The large hospital bed dwarfed her five-foot-eight frame and elevated her head. The breathing machine's swooshing and the heart monitor's steady beep were the only sounds in the room.

"Everything will be okay, baby. Just wake up." He held her hand and offered words of encouragement even though he wasn't sure she heard him.

"Mr. Morgan?" The doctor entered with a serious look on his face.

David rose from the chair, his pulse racing. "Yes, doctor. Have there been any changes since I spoke with you in the recovery room? How is she? Is she going to be all right?"

"Mr. Morgan, as I told you, we don't know right now. We did all we can. She suffered a lot of trauma. We've taken care of the internal bleeding and removed her spleen, so all we can do now is wait and hope." He glanced at her chart.

"Money isn't an issue, doctor. If you think she needs a specialist—"

"I assure you, Mr. Morgan, the surgical team consisted of the finest doctors. Now, only time will tell." The doctor patted David's shoulder, then turned and left the room.

Tears welled and David blinked them back. He turned to his wife and took her hand. "Taylor, darling, you can make it. I know you can. I'm going to be right here. Do you hear me? Squeeze my hand if you do."

Her fingers curled around his hand. The grip was weak, but she responded.

"Doctor, doctor!" David yelled. "Come quick. I think she's waking."

The doctor rushed back into the room.

David gazed at him, heart filled with hope. "She squeezed my hand. Squeeze it again, Taylor."

The physician put a stethoscope to her chest. He raised her bandage and lifted her eyelid. "Mrs. Morgan, if you can hear me, blink your eyes."

David watched her closely. She blinked, not once, but twice.

"That's good, Mrs. Morgan. You're doing fine, just fine. You've been in an accident and were badly hurt, but you're going to be okay. Your husband is here."

David stood and leaned in. "Hello, darling. I've been so worried about you, but like the doctor says, you're going to be fine."

He brushed a kiss against her cheek.

* * * *

You aren't Frank! Where's Frank? Why are you kissing me? I don't know you. Somebody help...

Who was this man? Mariah fluttered her eyes and barely lifted her head off the pillow. The mere movement caused her temple to pound. Her gaze darted around the room. Nothing looked familiar. Why did she feel so sore?

Nothing she saw made sense. Strange machines, dials, sounds, and the room—so white, so pristine. She tried to raise herself, but couldn't. Where was she?

Glancing down at the strange tube in her arm, she gasped, then raised her hand and touched her head. Bandaged? God help her. Where was her husband? Her mind formed Frank's name but her lips failed to speak it as darkness shrouded her.

* * * *

A woman in white stood over Mariah. "Oh, Mrs. Morgan, you're awake. We've been so worried about you. Your husband just went down to the cafeteria for something to eat. He's been here every day for the past two weeks. You gave us quite a scare."

The stranger fluffed Mariah's pillow and checked the tube in her arm. "Wouldn't you know you'd wake up the minute he left? Poor fellow, he's barely had time to change his clothes."

Cafeteria? The word meant nothing. Two weeks? She'd been here for two weeks? And where was *here*?

She tried to ask, but nothing came out. Vaguely recalling something thick and painful in her mouth, she swallowed. Thank goodness whatever had been there was gone.

"Don't try to speak, Mrs. Morgan." The stranger patted her arm. "Your throat is probably pretty raw. We just took the breathing tube out yesterday. You'll be able to talk soon, but now you just need to rest and get well. Let me give you a little more pain medication." She fiddled with some sort of bagged liquid hanging above the bed. Her fingers followed the tube down and smoothed the tape holding a needle in Mariah's arm. "There, that should make you feel a little more comfortable."

Breathing tube? Mrs. Morgan? What's happening? Somebody tell me, please. Confused and frightened, Mariah's teary eyes focused on the man who walked through the door.

"Ah, Mr. Morgan, your wife is finally awake." The woman in white greeted him. "She seems pretty alert."

"Taylor, sweetheart." He rushed to the bed. "Thank God, you're awake. I've been so worried about you."

Mariah turned her head to the side, avoiding the stranger's kiss. "I'm not Taylor." Her words were merely a whisper that no one heard.

"What are you trying to say, darling?" He bent lower.

"I asked her not to try to speak yet." The white-clad woman rubbed her own throat. "The breathing tube you know."

"Of course." He nodded. "The nurse is right. Don't talk, sweetie. When you're healed, we'll have lots of time to chat. Just rest."

Confusion shrouded Mariah. Why did they keep calling her Mrs. Morgan, and mentioning Taylor? Why weren't they using her own name?

A tear slid down her cheek. She'd rest for now, but when she could speak, she'd insist on knowing where she was and why a strange man considered her his wife.

The man she knew only as Mr. Morgan stretched his hands over his head then massaged the small of his back. "Now that I know you're on the mend, I'm going home to shower, shave and change clothes. Your parents are waiting for my call to update them on your condition. I'll be back tomorrow. You get some rest, baby." He bent and kissed her forehead.

Yes, go away. I need to think…and answers…I need some answers. Mariah sensed herself drifting off. Something made her very drowsy.

* * * *

The nurse's poking and prodding rudely awakened Mariah. "Good morning, Mrs. Morgan. I need to check your vitals."

Sunlight barely filtered through whatever covered the window. Mariah's head felt like it hovered somewhere above her. She blinked, hoping she was in the middle of a bad dream and about to wake up.

A strange band squeezed her arm, and she grimaced. The nurse placed a round, flat object against Mariah's skin, and appeared to listen intently. "Good blood pressure, Mrs. Morgan," she finally said. "How are you feeling?"

How? Terrified! Mariah heard her own heartbeat. "I'm sore," was all she could croak out.

"Of course you're sore. You were in a terrible car accident." She jotted something on a board of some sort.

Mariah's thoughts jumbled, and putting them into words proved impossible. What kind of accident was a *car?* Where was her family?

The nurse rounded the bed and revealed the shortness of her skirt. Mariah widened her eyes and bit her lip to keep her mouth from gaping. How inappropriate to show so much leg.

The woman tucked the covers in at the end of the metal frame. "Do you think you could manage a drink this morning? Perhaps some ginger ale? The doctor left orders for you to have liquids. Once we know you can tolerate drinking, perhaps we can get you a food tray."

Mariah *was* hungry. If she'd been here for two weeks, how had she survived without eating? Just the mere thought of being without food for so long made her stomach growl. "Yes… please." She forced out the words.

After the nurse placed a filled glass on Mariah's tray, she pushed a button on the side of the bed. Mariah rose into a sitting position. Her gaze darted from the mechanism to the nurse, and questions burned in her mind. How had she done that?

Amidst jumbled thoughts, she maneuvered around the tube in her arm and picked up the glass, anxious to ease the soreness of her throat. As she took a sip, *he* entered the room.

"Taylor! Look at you. Sitting up! You must be feeling better."

The man called David Morgan had combed his blond hair and shaved. He didn't look nearly as haggard as she recalled. Not quite as tall as her Frank, the shirt he wore revealed the same muscular shoulders.

Mariah considered him good-looking, but his clothes, his shoes... everything about him and this place seemed strange. Everyone dressed and spoke differently. If only someone would explain what was happening.

"It won't be long before I can take you home, babe."

David Morgan interrupted her thoughts. "I'll bet you'll be happy to be back in your own home and bed."

Mariah's hand trembled. She set her glass down, lay back against her pillow and looked away. Why would she go home with him? She didn't even know the man.

Using every bit of mustered strength, she turned her glaring gaze back to him. "I'm *not* Taylor!" she croaked.

CHAPTER THREE

Colorado Territory--1872

Taylor's head pounded with pain. Trying to focus, she opened her eyes and blinked a few times, then propped herself up on her elbows. Everything looked foreign. The room was bright and cheery, but things appeared very old fashioned. She fingered the patchwork quilt covering the bed, and puzzled over the antique mirror hanging above an old-time washbowl and pitcher across the room. An incessant ache throbbed in her temple.

Where was she? What'd happened to her? A zillion questions raced through her mind.

"David!" Her call for her husband resonated pain in her head. "Where are you?"

She slid off the bed. Her legs wavered beneath her, and she clung to the bedpost for a time. After regaining her equilibrium, she weaved across the room and peered into the mirror. A massive bandage covered the top her head; black circles ringed her swollen eyes. She didn't recognize herself.

"Boy, I look like hell," she muttered.

As she raised her hand to touch the bandage, the door behind her opened, and she spied the reflection of an unknown man.

"Mariah, sweetheart. You're finally awake." He crossed the room with open arms.

Taylor spun and faced him. Feeling disoriented, she

shook her head. "You have the wrong room, sir."

His brows arched. "Mariah, what are you talking about? What wrong room?"

"Look fella, I'm not Mariah. Evidently you're in the wrong place if you are looking for someone by that name."

The stranger rushed over and took her in his arms. "Oh my sweet angel, the bump on your head is worse than Doc Samuels thought."

Taylor shoved him away. "Take your hands off me. Who is Doc Samuels, and *who* in the hell are you?"

Suddenly, the room spun. Her stomach turned queasy. Needing to sit, she staggered back to the bed, her gaze still assessing the stranger.

"I'm Frank… your husband." He followed her, his head cocked, his eyes clouded in confusion.

She swallowed. "Excuse me? My husband's name is David… David Morgan. I don't know who you are, mister, but you must be the one who bumped *your* head if you think I'm your wife."

"Well, if you aren't, then just who might you be?"

"Taylor Morgan. I live in Denver. Can you please tell me where I am?"

"You're in Colorado, about two hours from Denver City. Don't you remember?"

"Two hours? How in the hell did I get here?"

Frank's eyes widened. "When did you start cussin'?"

"Don't worry about it, just answer me. How did I get here?" Her last nerve frayed, and he plucked at it.

"Don't you recall? We were going to town in the wagon—"

"Wagon? What the hell would I be doing in a station wagon?"

Frank took a deep breath. "I ain't got a clue 'bout no station wagon, but we were going to town, and Jacob needed to pee. I think he disturbed some rattlesnakes and they spooked the horses... Sound familiar?"

Taylor's mind raced. Who was this loony? "Who is Jacob? Wagon? What horses? I don't know what you're talking about. Frank... is it? Look, *Frank*, I have an idea. Why don't you just call me a cab and I'll get out of your way."

She looked down at the tacky nightgown she wore and wondered who had removed her clothing. Tugging at the sack-like shift, she let out an exasperated huff. "If you'll just retrieve my things, I'll get dressed and be ready to go when the taxi gets here."

* * * *

Frank felt totally bewildered. *Taxi? Cab?* He wasn't surprised she didn't remember the events leading to her injury, but he *was* shocked she'd created a new personality for herself. "Look, Mariah, uh... Taylor, you've been in and out of consciousness for almost two weeks now. Doc Samuels visits almost every day to check on you. Now, you just lay down and I'll send for him."

Taylor shot him a puzzled stare. "Why would a doctor make a house call? If I was injured, why am I not in a hospital?"

"Hospital? Doc Samuels is all we have around these parts. We always send for Doc when someone is hurt. Now, try to stay calm until he gets here. In the meantime, can I have Callie fix you something' to eat? You must be starvin'."

Taylor squared her shoulders and winced. Massaging her temples with her fingertips, she took a deep breath. "Look, Frank, or whatever your name is. I don't know any Callie, and I don't know what you're trying to pull, but it's not working. Don't *piss me* off. Either call me a taxi or bring me the damn phone!"

Her anger and continued cussing stunned him. "Can we just wait until Doc Samuels gets here and checks you out? Please? Lay down and rest."

She rolled her eyes. "Okay, I guess it wouldn't hurt. I don't feel very well. My head throbs with every heartbeat, and I feel woozy. *But* after I've rested a bit, I'm outta here." She leaned back on the pillow.

"That's a good girl." He picked up her feet, swiveled them around to the bed. "I'll send someone for the doctor."

Frank raced out of the room, closing the door behind him. He paused in the hallway and leaned against the wall, trying to make sense of what had just happened. There was no logic to it. He made his way downstairs and headed for the bunkhouse and his foreman, passing his daughter without saying a word.

"Lloyd, Lloyd!" Frank yelled. "You need to get to town quick and get Doc Samuels out here. Something's not right with the missus."

Callie waited on the porch, concern etched on her face. She looked so much like her mother, same reddish hair and big green eyes. "Pa, what's wrong. Is it Ma? Is she worse?"

He grasped her shoulders. "Callie honey, I have to be honest with you. I'm really worried about your ma. She woke up and doesn't know who she is. She doesn't even know *me*! Far as I can tell, she thinks she's somebody else—someone named Taylor something."

"Are you sure?"

"Believe me, this is no joke. Maybe if you went upstairs, she might recognize you."

Callie turned to go, but he grabbed her arm. "No, maybe that's not a good idea. Perhaps it'd be better if you and Jacob gave Ma a few more days to rest. She's still not feline' well." Was he making the right decision? He wrestled with his indecisiveness. Recalling Mariah's temper display and continued use of bad language, he nodded. "Yep, that's probably the best idea. Let her sleep until Doc Samuels gets here."

Frank shoved his hands into his pockets and paced the length of the porch.

Callie stepped in front of him. "Pa, don't worry. She'll be fine. It's just that bad bump on her head… isn't it?" A deep crease furrowed his daughter's brow. "She will be all right, won't she, Pa?"

Frank put his arm around her. "I'll make you a deal, honey. If you don't worry, then I won't. Doc Samuels will fix her up as good as new."

"Worry 'bout what, Pa?" Jacob jumped onto the porch, his hair tousled and dirt smudged on his cheek.

"It's nothing important, son." Frank lied through his teeth. His stomach was already in a knot and he feared the worst.

CHAPTER FOUR

Denver, Colorado—2002

David sat in the chair next to his wife's hospital bed. His jaw twitched in response to her denial. "What do you mean you aren't Taylor? Of course, you are."

Mariah shook her head and whispered, "No, I'm not! *My* name is Mariah Cassidy."

Her seriousness worried him. "Fine, sweetheart. Whatever you say. You rest and I'll go get the nurse or a doctor or… somebody."

He cast a final confused look over his shoulder as he walked out the door.

Mariah took another sip of ginger ale. The bubbles tickled her nose and eased her dry throat. She needed to talk—she had questions—lots of them. The main one: why in the world a stranger considered her his wife. She glanced around the room, hoping something would strike a familiar cord. It didn't.

He returned with the doctor, and pointed at her. "Dr. Shaw, please calm my wife. Tell her what you told me."

"Mrs. Morgan," Dr. Shaw approached the bed. His spectacles rested halfway down a pointy nose, his gray hair looked as though someone had greased it to his head. "I think you should know that some memory impairment is expected from the type of trauma you suffered."

Mariah tried to sit straighter but winced at the pain. "My memory is just fine. I know perfectly well who I am. My name is Mariah Cassidy. I don't know this man and I don't know you. I don't even know *where* I am." She wanted to scream.

Tears welled in her eyes.

Dr. Shaw rested his hand on her shoulder. "Calm down, Mrs. Morgan. You're in Saint Anthony's Hospital in Denver. You've been in a serious car accident. It may take a while, but everything will come back to you. Just give yourself time."

Frustration welled and caught in Mariah's throat. Why did everyone believe her to be Taylor Morgan? Something was terribly wrong. She didn't understand who or what this 'car' thing was they keep talking about, but before she could voice her thoughts, the doctor walked to the machine on the other side of her bed. "Here, let me give you something to calm you a little."

He inserted a needle into the tube in her arm, and a dark void pulled at her. "Wait. Wai..."

* * * *

David massaged his brow. "Doctor, are you sure she's going to be all right?"

"Mr. Morgan, like I told your wife, you have to allow time for her to heal. It's not at all unusual for someone who has suffered a head trauma to have memory loss. She'll be fine." He picked up the chart at the foot of the bed and jotted something down, then glanced up. "Do yourself a favor, Mr. Morgan. Go home and get some rest."

David looked at his sleeping wife. Longing for a nap himself, he nodded. "I guess you're right. I could stand a break.

Will she be out long?"

"She'll sleep for the rest of the day. Why don't you come back this evening?"

David lifted his wife's limp hand, kissed it and whispered, "I'll be back later, darling. Sleep well."

* * * *

Mariah fought to open her eyes. Blinking to adjust to the room's darkness, she saw only dim shades of orange and red filtering around the window. She assumed the sun must be setting.

Looking around, she determined she was alone. Trying to sit upright, she propped herself on one hand.

"Yes, Mrs. Morgan. You rang? What can I do for you?" The voice from nowhere startled her.

Searching for the source, Mariah surveyed the room. Was there a ghost haunting her now?

"Mrs. Morgan. Are you there?"

Straining, Mariah forced herself into a sitting position. "Ye…yes, I'm here, but where *are* you?" Her voice trembled as her gaze roamed the room.

"I'm at the nurse's station, Mrs. Morgan. You pushed your call button. What do you need?"

Mariah raised her hand and saw the device beneath her palm. As if scalded by hot water, she jerked away. "I'm sorry, I didn't know about the… the button."

"Are you sure you don't need anything? If not, we'll be in soon to check your vitals."

Vitals? There was that word again. Mariah wondered what it meant. She wondered if it had something to do with why they kept coming into her room and poking at her.

Being careful of the tube in her arm, she dropped her legs over the side of the bed and sat for a moment. Her head pounded, keeping beat with her heart. "I need to get up, but *how* if I'm connected to this horrid contraption," she mumbled.

If only she could look out the window, maybe she'd see something familiar.

The nurse came in just as Mariah prepared to stand. "Oh nooooo, Mrs. Morgan. It's much too soon for you to be up. You put those toes right back under the covers. We took your catheter tube out, but if you need to use the bathroom, it's the bedpan for now."

Mrs. Morgan, Mrs. Morgan. I'm not Mrs. Morgan. Mariah's mind screamed but the words lodged in her throat.

Catheter? Bedpan? Each time someone spoke, they created yet another question in her mind. Her shoulders sagging with the weight of her confusion, she obediently put her feet back upon the bed and allowed the nurse to pull the covers over her.

"That's a good girl. Now, let's check that temperature." The white-clad woman stuck a pencil-length device in Mariah's ear. "Good, ninety-eight point six on the nose."

Placing her finger where the object had just been, Mariah checked to make sure nothing remained inside. "What was that?"

"Oh, you haven't seen the newest thermometer?" The woman held it up. "This little gem is certainly better than the one you held under your tongue for three minutes." She jotted some notes on a piece of paper then looked up at Mariah. "Say, sounds like your voice is getting stronger, Mrs. Morgan. How's your throat feeling?"

Mariah massaged the front of her neck. "Much better.

It's still sore, but at least I can talk."

After wrapping the strange-looking contraption around Mariah's upper arm again, the woman squeezed the little bulb until the band grew uncomfortably tight. She then placed the small, circular disc on the inner side of Mariah's elbow.

"What's that you're doing now?"

Mariah received an annoyed look in return. "Shhh," the nurse commanded with authority. "I need to hear your pulse."

Mariah didn't dare utter a sound and waited until the woman straightened again. "Are you through?"

"Yes, Mrs. Morgan. Your temp and blood pressure are fine. Now that you're able to take fluids orally, let's get that nasty old tube out of your arm. It looks like you're on the mend. Mr. Morgan should be able to take you home in a few days."

The hair on the back of Mariah's neck bristled at the thought. She snuggled deeper into her pillows and wondered to which home she was going. She gazed to the ceiling. *Please, God, let it be the Rocking C.*

"There, no more annoying tube." The nurse interrupted Mariah's thoughts of her beloved ranch. "Would you like to watch some TV?"

Mariah rubbed the crook of her arm, relieved to be able to move it freely. "Watch what?"

"TV, you know… television?"

"No, I'm sorry, I don't know what that is."

The nurse pointed at a square box suspended in the corner. "Wow, you really are suffering from memory loss. That's the television." She approached the bedside table, pulled out the drawer and handed Mariah an object. "Here's the remote control."

She took it. What did it do, and why would one watch a black box with a glass front? She studied the mysterious thing then cast a puzzled look at her attendant.

The nurse took back what she called the remote, aimed it in the direction of the box and pushed a button. The image of a man appeared on the screen. Mariah heard him talking. She stiffened and leaned back against the bed. Was he speaking to her? Trying to make sense of all the strange happenings made her head hurt.

When the nurse pushed another button, the screen immediately changed to a man kissing a woman. She depressed the button again—a person cooking, then someone talking about feminine hygiene. Mariah's mouth gaped. Why would they discuss such a private thing? This thing called a remote surely was a product of the devil himself.

The nurse handed the control back to Mariah. "Ring if there's anything you need, Mrs. Morgan." The woman left the room.

Being called Mrs. Morgan didn't faze Mariah—she busied herself pushing buttons. Suddenly the sound got very loud; it hurt her ears. Mariah frantically searched to find a way to lower it before the nurse came back to scold her. Fumbling with the buttons, she found the right one and sighed.

Undaunted, she scanned the channels, searching for the kissing couple, but they were gone. Instead, she found a big yellow singing bird. She settled back against her pillow and watched with wide eyes. If only Frank was here. Maybe he could help her understand all this.

* * * *

The orderly removed her dinner tray just as David returned. He brushed her forehead with a kiss. "Hello, darling. I'm glad to see you're awake."

Although she stiffened at his show of affection, she noticed how good he smelled. Clean, yet a little like the sweet-smelling toilet water she bought at the mercantile. She still struggled to understand why this man insisted he knew her—and all too well, apparently. Her earlier statement about her identity seemed to trouble him. She hesitated to upset him again, at least until she had a chance to set things right.

"I just ate." She picked a safe topic.

"How was it? You know what they say about hospital food." David took off his coat and sat next to her bed.

"It was good. I enjoyed it." She didn't know who *they* were or what *they* said.

"The nurse tells me you tried to get out of bed."

"I'm tired of lying here. I just wanted to look out the window." She pulled her mouth into a pout.

David laughed. "You were never a good sick person, Taylor. Too darn impatient."

There he goes with that Taylor thing again. Enough is enough!

"David... uh... David, is it? We need to discuss why you think I'm Taylor. I assume since you share the same last name, she's your wife."

David's eyes widened and his mouth dropped. He leapt to his feet and looked deep into her eyes. "Taylor! I don't *think*, I *know* who you are. You *are* my wife! I've been married to you for over five years now. You look like my wife, you sound like her and you carry a driver's license that told the police you are Taylor Morgan. That's why they called me."

"Police? Driver's license? Your wife? This isn't making any sense at all. You're scaring me." Mariah covered her face with her hands.

David put a hand on her shoulder. "Honey, don't cry. Maybe if we try going back to when the accident happened, you might remember." He sat, his brow furrowed. "I hope this works."

Mariah brushed away her tears and took a deep breath. "I'm willing to try anything." She chewed her bottom lip while she thought hard about the last thing she recalled. "Hmmm, I remember waking up, getting dressed, waking up the kids—"

"*What kids?*" His eyes wide, David almost toppled his chair.

"Jacob and Callie, of course." His reaction stunned her into silence.

Eyeing her while grasping the chair arms, he sat straighter. "Go on."

"All right." She lapsed into thought, shutting her eyes and massaging her brow to summon memories. "Then, after breakfast we all got into the wagon to go into town." She opened her eyes. "That's the last thing I remember." A shrug of her shoulders caused her to grimace at the pain.

David leaned over and rubbed her hand. "You poor darling. You're all confused."

Mariah jerked away. "I'm *not* confused. You seem to be the one who's befuddled. If you could just find Frank, I'm sure he'll explain everything."

David patted her hand. "Okay, sweetheart. You try to get some rest, and I'll see if I can find...Frank."

He donned his coat. "Goodnight, sweetheart, I-I'll be back tomorrow."

Tension ridged his jaw, but thankfully he didn't kiss her.

The moment he left, her body relaxed. She turned

onto her side and fluffed her pillow. If only she could fall asleep, maybe when she woke, this bad dream would all be over. Unfortunately, her gaze rested focused on the remote control atop the table, and her hand snaked out and grabbed it. Thoughts of finding a mirror to see what David Morgan saw were lost with the wonder of the amazing black box.

Now let's see. I push this button.

CHAPTER FIVE

Colorado Territory--1872

Taylor opened her eyes to a room engulfed in black. Wondering how long she'd slept, she raised her stiff and sore body into a sitting position. She dangled her feet over the side of the bed and stood. "Okay, legs, don't fail me now."

Her eyes adjusted to the darkness, and shuffled toward the slice of light on the floor. She slapped the wall in search of a light switch, but felt none. Frustration tightened her chest, but she found the knob and opened the door just enough to peek out. A flickering lamp sat on a small, doily-covered table in an empty hallway.

She eased the door shut. If she planned to explore, she couldn't do it in her nightgown. Crossing back to the bed, she grabbed the robe hanging on the post. Her arms felt leaden as she lifted them and slid them through the sleeves. She winced in pain, but pulled the wrapper around her then tiptoed out to the railing at the top of the stairs and looked over.

Taking each stair gingerly, she made her way down into the dimly lit room. She heard voices and followed the sound to the kitchen doorway and peered around the corner into brightness. The man, Frank, and two children sat at the table. The delicious smell drifting from fried chicken heaped on a plate made Taylor's stomach rumble. This wasn't a time to let anger get in the way of sustenance. She pasted a smile on her face and rounded the corner. "Good evening. May I join you?"

Frank pushed his chair back so quickly he almost dumped himself onto the floor. He gulped down his mouthful of food and stood. "Yes! Please, join us," he sputtered.

He pulled the chair out at the end of the table and retrieved another place setting. In his haste, he almost overturned the lamp on the counter.

Taylor sat and pulled a napkin into her lap. She surveyed the delicious-looking fare on the table and waited for someone to pass a dish. For a moment, no one spoke. The young boy she assumed to be Jacob, bent over his plate, shoveling food into his mouth like he'd been starved for a week. After swallowing a forkful, he looked up and grinned at her. "Gee, Ma, I'm glad you're better. Pa said you weren't feelin' very good."

She tensed. First a strange man claimed to be her husband, and now a scruffy kid called her 'Ma.' What next? Taylor squared her shoulders. "Young man, I am *not* your ma. I'm... Well some of us are a bit confused about who I am exactly." She cocked her head and glared at Frank. "I'm not sure right now where I am or why I'm here, but I do know for a fact that I do *not* have children, and I *am* extremely hungry. I would appreciate being able to have a bite to eat without being hassled any further."

Jacob's eyebrows knitted into one and his lips pulled into a frown. His lip quivering, he looked at his father. Frank gave a quick shake of his head, and Jacob stared at his plate and fell silent.

"May... may...I be excused?" The girl, visibly fighting back tears, didn't wait for an answer. She bolted out of her chair and up the stairs.

Jacob's gaze snapped up and his eyes widened. "Can I go too, Pa?"

"Sure, son, go ahead."

The room fell silent. Frank cleared his throat. "Ahem, Mariah... Now wait, before you bite my head off for callin' you by your name, please hear me out."

Taylor stared at him. "Well?"

"I know you've been in an accident and things are real confusin' right now, but you have to think of the children. They don't understand what's going on any more than I do. You almost bit Jacob's head off 'cause he asked how you felt. Now, I'm more than willin' to give you as much time as you need to remember who I am, but can you please, at least, act like you know your own kids. Callie and Jacob need their mother."

Mother? Taylor took a deep, calming breath. "Look, Frank, I don't mean to hurt your kids or you for that matter, but I don't understand what's happening here. My last memory was leaving for work, and today I'm sitting at an unfamiliar table with a strange man and two children who claim to be my family. I don't even know what day it is. What can I do to convince you I'm not this Mariah person? I'm Taylor Morgan. I live at 1444 Broadshire Lane in Denver. I'm married to David Morgan. Have been for five years, and I've never had a child. If I had, *don't* you think I'd know about it?"

Frank's lips narrowed, and he rested his hands on either side of his plate. She expected him to spring from his chair, but instead, he took in a deep breath and held it, then loudly exhaled. "What say we take this a step at a time? For the children's sake, until we figure this out, can I at least call you Mariah when they're around?"

"I suppose I can handle that, but just don't get used to it. I'm Taylor and that's all there is to it."

He nodded. "Fine, *Taylor,* maybe we need to back-paddle a bit here. Can I tell you what happened and see if it sounds at all familiar?"

His evident frustration mirrored her own. Since she didn't have a better idea, she nodded. "I'm just as anxious as you are to straighten out this mess. I'm listening."

He stood, put his hands in his pockets and began pacing. A wave of loneliness washed over Taylor. David always did the same thing when he was nervous.

"Two weeks ago we started for town." He stopped and gazed at her. "Remember? You were sitting on the front porch having coffee when I rode in from the pasture. You said you were going to pack a basket..." He stopped and looked at her, clearly desperate for a reaction.

Listening to Frank was like having someone read her a story. Taylor pitched forward, anxious to see how it ended. "Go on."

He began pacing again. "A nest of rattlers spooked the horses and the team took off on a dead run. The wagon hit a rock and flipped over. You hit your head when you were thrown out and were unconscious until yesterday." He sagged back into his chair and grasped the table's edge. "Now you tell me you aren't Mariah. Can you understand why I'm confused? Do you remember any of this?"

He looked so distraught, a pang of sympathy stabbed at her. She shook her head. "I'm sorry, but none of that sounds even remotely familiar. I wish I could explain this all away, but I can't be who I'm not. I have a husband somewhere who must wonder where the hell I am."

Frank's knuckles turned white as his fingers tightened

on the table. "You have to remember something, Mariah... Taylor. Please."

She leaned forward, rested on her elbows, and rubbed her forehead. "Let's see. I got up late—I'm always late. David hates that about me. Anyway, I recall driving down Center Street on my way to an important meeting." She tapped her brow in an effort to force the memories to come. "The radio... I was in a hurry. I heard squealing tires. That's all I remember until you came into the room upstairs."

"Center Street? Squealing tires? Radio?" He repeated each word as if they were a foreign language. A puzzled look shot from his eyes. He cocked his head to one side and stared at her for a few moments before asking, "Taylor, you say you were driving to a meeting. What exactly were you driving?"

"My Lexus."

"What's a Lex us?"

"A top-of-the-line automobile."

"What's an auto mobile?"

"Oh, come on. You've gotta be kidding."

"I'm serious. I have no idea what those things are."

Taylor leaned back in her chair and covered her face. "Okay. If this isn't *Candid Camera*, I must be in the *Twilight Zone*."

Frank didn't speak, but his furrowed brow and questioning gaze indicated total confusion.

Unlike her usual stoic self, Taylor's shoulders sagged and a tear slipped down her cheek. "How can I make you understand?"

He touched her hand. "Maybe if I show you around, something might jog your memory."

Frank took her hand and led her into a large room. "This is our parlor. You took such care in decorating it. Does it look familiar?"

Taylor wrinkled her nose at the archaic style. She pulled her hand free from his and fingered the velvet settee with intricate woodwork and button tufting. Straight back mahogany chairs—one with arms, the other a side chair—both covered in ungodly brocade sat on either side. "God no! Give me oak and leather any day. This certainly isn't my taste in decor."

He picked up a kerosene lamp and ushered her out the back door. "Remember the porch I built for you? You love to sit out here and enjoy the peace and quiet. You always say it's your escape from Callie and Jacob's bickerin'."

Along the wall of the house, a small table separated two wicker rocking chairs with well-worn seat cushions. Taylor walked to the railing and inhaled the fragrant honeysuckle. She looked at the half moon, sitting low in the sky and at the outline of the barn across the way. How often had Mariah—whoever she was—sat here?

Taylor stared into space. "It doesn't look familiar, but it sure is nice. I love honeysuckle."

Frank walked over, plucked a blossom and handed it to her. "You always loved honeysuckle. That's why I planted it all along the railing. Let's sit for minute. Maybe things are starting to come back."

He sounded encouraged, but she didn't want to give him false hope. She needed some time to process everything. Lowering herself into a chair, she started rocking. After a long sigh, she glanced up at him. "I sure could go for a cup of coffee."

"I'll get you one. There's a pot on the stove." The squeaking kitchen door caused the crickets to cease chirping.

Taylor stopped rocking, waiting for them to resume

their melodic song. Used to noisy city life, it had been a long time since she'd been anywhere so quiet. She scanned the property's moonlit perimeter, glanced along the length of the porch, then back at the house. *Whoever you are, Mariah, you've got quite a home... and husband.*

Frank returned with a steaming cup of coffee and placed it on the table next to the lantern. "There you go, just like you like it. A little milk and sugar." His cheek dimpled with his smile.

Taylor gulped. "How did you know I like my coffee that way?" Her mind seized. *Don't panic, Taylor. It's just a coincidence.*

"I've fixed your coffee hundreds of times in the seventeen years we've been married."

"Seventeen years?"

He sat in the chair across the table from her. "Yes. You were sixteen when we got engaged and eighteen when we married. Remember? I always joked about my saving you from being an old maid." His gaze roamed her face. "I have to say, you're even more beautiful now than when I married you."

Taylor wished for a mirror as a thousand thoughts ran through her mind. She began rocking again, trying to sort through them. *Seventeen years?* She tried to compute the numbers and shook her head. "This doesn't add up. I'm twenty-seven years old. If I married you seventeen years ago, I would have been ten. I married David when I was twenty-two. If you add seventeen years to that, you're trying to tell me I'm almost forty. That's ridiculous."

"Callie is fifteen and Jacob is ten. Try to remember. Callie was born at your parents' house and Jacob here... upstairs in the bedroom."

Taylor stopped rocking and straightened. "My parents.

That's it! My parents, Gladys and Howard Sturm, can prove who I am. Let's call them."

"Call? On who? Those people aren't your parents."

"Of course they are. Now you're acting ridiculous… like I wouldn't know my own mother and father. Just call them." She blew steam from the cup and sipped her coffee.

"What do you mean *call?*" Frank's brow arched. "They most likely don't live nearby. Besides it's far to late to visit."

"Call them. Telephone! Pick up the receiver, dial the number!" Her jaw tensed at his feigned stupidity.

"Sweetie, you're scaring me. I don't know what a tel a fone is."

"How can you not know? Even if you don't have one, I'm sure there's one somewhere. A public phone maybe? You could drive me there." She put her cup on the table and stood.

"I can't drive you anywhere just yet. I haven't fixed the wheels on the wagon, and Ma has the buggy."

Taylor stomped her foot. "I don't want to go in a wagon or a buggy! How about your car? Surely you have one."

"You keep mentioning that word, but I don't know what a car is." He peered up at her, his brow creased and confusion clouding his eyes.

"A car. A vehicle. An automobile. You know… four tires, an engine. Preferably a sporty sedan with class. This is just unfriggin-believable."

"Nope, no car. Haven't ever seen one of those, nor heard tell of one. Sounds interestin' though." He folded his hands across his stomach, slowly shaking his head.

Taylor's temples ached. "We aren't getting anywhere, and I'm really tired. I think I'll just go up to bed. We can talk more in the morning."

"That's a good idea. I'm feelin' a might tired myself."

She held her breath. *Oh my God, he thinks I'm his wife. Surely he won't want to sleep in the same room.*

"I'll be in the guest room if you need me."

Taylor exhaled. When Frank stood, picked up the lamp, and opened the door, she stepped inside.

He paused to inspect the noisy hinges. "I've gotta put some grease to this thing tomorrow." After closing the door, he followed her upstairs.

Taylor relied on the banister for support—each step reminding her of her injuries. When she reached her bedroom, she glanced over her shoulder to assure Frank went into the room across the hall. She closed her door and leaned against it. *If I dropped acid, at least that would explain this really bad trip I'm on.*

CHAPTER SIX

Denver, Colorado—2002

Mariah grew tired of watching television—too many things to try to understand. She lay awake in the semi-darkness of her hospital room. The nurses finished their nightly ritual and left her in peace. She stared at flashes of light reflecting through the window and watched the colors dance across the ceiling tiles. Unusual sounds coming from beyond the window piqued her curiosity. Did she dare get up?

She edged to the bedside, lowered her legs and searched for the floor. The bed was too high; her bare feet dangled in the air. She sat for a moment and pondered her actions. What if someone caught her? Would she get into trouble? Was she strong enough to stand? There seemed only one way to tell.

She slid off the bed and braced herself against the mattress to test the sturdiness of her legs and listened to make sure no one was coming. When she felt steady, she shuffled across the floor to the window. The cold tile stung the soles of her feet.

The bendable metal that created a unique curtain created another strange thing to ponder. She pushed two thin slats apart and peered through them. Her breath caught and she widened her eyes.

The flashing lights came from a large sign mounted atop a tall building across the way. "This Bud's For You" blinked off and on in bright red letters. The words held no meaning at all. Holding her head, she peered down to the street below. Shock sent her reeling backwards.

"Oh, my Lord." She covered her mouth and stood frozen in place.

She inched back for another look. How in the world could she be so high in the air? Dots of bright white and red lights darted in various directions and made her queasy. She raised her gaze and looked left then right, awed by the tall structures that spiked the air like giant fence posts. What were the strange moving lights below, and how did the buildings get so tall? She swallowed hard, unable to find an explanation that made sense.

Now, even more questions muddled her mind, and she had no one to ask. She hurried back to bed and crawled under the covers. Her head spun and her heart pounded. Had she gone mad? It seemed a long time before exhaustion calmed her mind and allowed sleep to claim her.

* * * *

Mariah awoke to David bending over her and kissing her forehead. Again, her body stiffened in response to another unwelcome show of affection. Earlier, she'd wanted someone to talk to, but now she wasn't in the mood. It had been late when she finally fell asleep, and the nurses had already disturbed her once. With a deep breath, she pushed herself into a semi-sitting position, intending to be cordial. Her mouth widened into a big yawn, and she stretched her arms up in the air until soreness forced them down. "Morning." She smacked her lips at the pasty taste in her mouth.

"Good morning, Sunshine. Did you sleep well?" David seemed perky.

"Actually, I didn't. I'm more confused than ever."

"What about, honey?"

She feared telling him she'd gotten out of bed, but there was no other way to ask her questions without confessing. "About what's out there." She pointed toward the window.

"Outside?" He glanced to the blinds then back at her.

"I looked out last night because I wanted to see what caused the lights." She paused and waited for his explanation.

"Taylor, sweetie, you know you aren't supposed to be out of bed yet. Not until the doctor says."

Mariah bristled at his continuing use of endearing terms and the strange name, but didn't mention it. At the moment, getting the answers she needed was more important than anything else. "David, help me understand where I am."

"You're in St. Anthony's Hospital. The doctor told you that. Don't you remember?"

"I know that, but all around me are things I don't understand, things I've never seen before."

"Give me an example." He cocked his head and stared at her.

"You, the moving lights outside, the tall buildings, the roads, this place… all the strange contraptions. I don't recognize any of this."

He grasped her hand. "The doctor said it would take time."

She recoiled from his touch. "Time? How much time? Not remembering you is one thing, but how could I forget buildings and those light things? What are they? I hear squealing like suffering pigs, and other sounds I can't even describe. I've never heard them before in my life. How could a body forget all that?" Her mouth went dry.

"I don't know what you mean." His brow furrowed. "I want to help you remember, but show me what you're talking about. Let me help you to the window."

He lifted her off the bed and she didn't struggle. For a moment, being in his arms offered a feeling of security, but they weren't Frank's, and the sensation faded as fast as it'd surfaced. She stiffened.

David wasn't her husband, and she couldn't pretend differently. If she had memory loss, why was everything about her family so fresh in her mind?

He carried her across the room and placed her in a chair. With a yank on a string, he caused the slats to collapse and rise to the top of the window. She stared up, her mouth agape.

Afraid to look out, she hesitated, but David helped her stand. Her fingers gripped the sill as she forced herself to peer through the glass. Daylight had erased all the colored lights from last night. The large sign was now just words and a picture of a beautiful woman holding a glass of yellow liquid. Mariah glanced at the street below. No moving lights, now just a myriad of darting colors. Still, what she saw made no sense.

"Those, those." She clung to the sash with one hand and pointed to the objects below with the other. "What *are* those?"

David shot her a worried look. "Do you mean the cars? " He slowly shook his head. "Oh, sweetheart, maybe we shouldn't wait for the doctor. If you are trying to tell me you don't remember what a car is, this is a little more memory loss than I suspected."

Mariah turned from the window and stomped her foot. "Don't you think if I'd seen something like this before that I'd remember? Why won't you believe me? There is nothing wrong with my memory. My name is Mariah Cassidy. My husband's name is Frank. I have two children, and I live on the Rocking C Ranch."

David wrung his hands for a moment before patting her shoulder. "Wait right here. I'm going to ask the nurse to call the doctor. We need to sit down and discuss your prognosis. I'll be right back."

She was near tears when he left the room. How could she get him to listen? She turned back to the window and stared at the sky. *Please, Lord, tell me what day this is. How long have I been here?* She walked back to the bed and climbed in. Rolling to her side, she pulled her knees up to her chest and wrapped her arms around her legs. She wanted to sleep, wake up and have everything be as she remembered. A tear rolled down her cheek and splashed onto the pillow. "Oh, Frank, my darling Frank, where are you?"

* * * *

She kept her back to David when he returned. Although she didn't want him to see her cry, her sniffling gave her away.

"It's okay. Don't cry, honey. Dr. Shaw will be here soon. Maybe we can get some answers for you." David patted her hip in a gesture she considered far too familiar. She slid from beneath his touch and turned to face him. "What day is this? What year? How long have I been here?" Time had come for some answers.

"Maybe we should wait for the doctor." David's throat jiggled with a hard swallow.

"How long have I been here? I want to know!" Mariah's demand bordered on hysteria.

"Okay, okay." David displayed his palms in surrender. "Calm down. You've been here for almost three weeks. Today is May 28, 2002. Why?"

53

CHAPTER SEVEN

Colorado Territory--1872

"Oh shit, I'm still here!"

Taylor fell back against her pillow and sighed. If all this was some kind of joke, she didn't find it a bit funny. This morning, she'd hoped to wake up in her own bedroom next to the husband she knew. Her patience waned and her body tenses. Although Frank seemed nice, he wore on her nerves. Every time she asked for something, he pretended not to understand her meaning. As soon as she felt a little steadier on her feet, her first priority was to find the phone and call for a taxi. If only she could find her clothes. She sat on the bed's edge until she was able to stand.

Listening for footsteps and hearing none, she decided to explore the strange, antiquated room. She crossed to the armoire, and passing the mirror, glanced at her reflection. Her eyes were still discolored, but lighter hues of purple and yellow shone beneath them. She leaned in for a closer look. "It's funny how swollen eyes can make you look completely different. I don't even look like the same person."

Taylor started to open the armoire door, but an odd image flashed through her mind. What color hair had she just seen? Removing her hand from the knob, she took three steps backwards to the mirror. Her eyes widened and her mouth dropped. "*Red?*" She fingered the coppery strands. "I don't have red hair! Oh my God, this is so not funny."

"Frank! Frank," she screamed. "You get in here right now!" She opened the door "Frank," she hollered again. "Do you hear me?"

He climbed the stairs at a breathless pace, his cobalt blue eyes clouded with panic. "Heavenly days, Mariah. What's the matter?"

Taylor stomped her foot. "For the umpteenth time, my name is *not* Mariah, and this joke has gone far enough. Who in the hell dyed my hair?"

Frank seemed to ponder her question then rolled his eyes. "Is that what all this is about? For heaven sakes, you've always had red hair." His voice deepened in annoyance.

"Like hell I have." She looked around for something to throw. Not seeing anything she could readily pick up, she wagged a finger at him. "Now you listen to me. I like my blonde highlights and so does my husband. I *hate* red hair, and I'm getting really tired of this whole charade. I have better things to do with my time than play games. I have a life. I have a job. I'm pretty sure everyone wonders where in the hell I am. I don't expect you even called my office, did you?"

Frank stood toe-to-toe with her. The veins in his neck bulged. "Now looky here, lady. There's only so much a body can stand and I'm getting pretty gol' darned fed up with this myself. It's hard sittin' around and waiting' for you to get your memory back. The kids are haven' a pretty hard time with it, too. Because of your injuries, we missed the spring dance that Callie counted on. She was sorely disappointed, but that didn't keep her from worrying' about you none. We have lives, too, you know? That dance was important to her, but she didn't complain. Now, you repay all her worrying' by bein' rude. This isn't easy on any of us. We've all put everything on hold to take care of you and help you recover. I can't even let Jacob come up here because I don't want him exposed to your nasty temper and vile mouth."

"Nasty temper? Vile mouth? You haven't seen anything yet, buster." She scanned the room. "Where is my purse? I need to get my day planner out and find a phone number."

"There you go with that 'phone' thing again." His voice rose. "What ever it is, we *don't* have one. Get it through your head. And what the heck *is* a day planner?"

Exasperated, Taylor clomped to the armoire and yanked the door open. She glanced over her shoulder. "Would you leave? I'm getting dressed."

She turned back and couldn't believe what she saw. "What the hell kind of clothes are these?" She examined the length and fingered the cottony material. "What happened to the outfit I had on? I just bought it. It's a designer label, not one of these... these milkmaid costumes."

Frank had his hand on the doorknob, but he spun around and walked back to the center of the room. He glared at her. "Dadgummit, woman! You have me so confused and frustrated I don't even know what name to call you. Nothing you say makes any sense at all. You don't like anything around here, and you're just downright unpleasant. I'd send for the doc, but he can't do anything for hysterical women. Since he's due back here tomorrow to check on you, can we just make peace until then?"

Taylor clenched her fists, her anger matching Frank's, but she mellowed and threw her hands up in surrender. "Okay, okay. I'll wait for your doctor, although I doubt it's going to make any difference. *But,* tomorrow is the last day I'm putting up with this shit. I want my clothes and I want out of here."

She plopped on the bed and crossed her arms.

Frank marched back to the door, opened it, but glanced over his shoulder. "Go ahead and act like a sulking child if it helps. We'll see what the doc has to say tomorrow. In the meantime, I'd appreciate if you'd refrain from sin' cuss words. You never used them before and a filthy mouth really isn't ladylike." He walked out and closed the door before she had a chance to respond.

"Well, I never. How dare he tell me how to talk?" She pounded her fists into the soft, feather bed. "How dare he tell me to do anything! He's nothing to me."

She stopped and took a deep breath. *Calm down, Taylor. Breathe deeply.* She bent to peek under the bed, still searching for her purse. "Damn it, nothing but dust. Damn it, damn it, damn it."

"Do you hear me, Frank? I'm cussing," she yelled toward the door.

She slid off the bed, crossed to the mirror, bent in and examined her face. She ran fingers over lips that appeared much wider than she remembered. Maybe they were swollen like her eyes. Fingering her hair again, she sneered at her reflection. "God, I hate red. It even feels different…not as thick."

She glanced down at her body. The baggy nightgown she wore hid any curves she recalled. She pulled the waist tight and stood on tiptoes to see her reflection. Her breasts looked smaller. How strange.

Her stomach roiling, she sat back on the bed, rested her head in her hands and pondered all the strange things going on. Maybe someone in a higher position could help. She lifted her gaze to the ceiling. *Please, God. I know you may not know me very well, but I really need help right about now. I'm beginning to think I've gone crazy.*

****

A commotion sounded outside. Taylor pushed the curtain aside and peeked. Doc Samuels arrived in some weird-looking contraption right out of the musical, Oklahoma. She almost heard strains of the song, "Surrey with the Fringe on Top". She let the curtain fall back into place and plopped down on the bed. "Great! I wonder what kind of cornball remedy he'll come up with today," she grumbled.

Within minutes, Frank walked in with the doctor on his heels. "Look, dear, it's Doc Samuels."

Taylor clapped her hands in a mocking manner. "Oh goody, goody. Now I can get my memory back and go home."

Doc Samuels peered over the top of his spectacles. "Well, Missy, I see you're still having problems rememberin' things. Your husband tells me you've been acting a might bit stranger than before."

"Strange?" Taylor huffed. "I'll tell you what's strange. I've spent an enormous amount of precious time in this... this hole in the wall. There are no conveniences. I can't call home, I can't call work, my clothes are gone, and some asshole dyed my hair red."

The doctor's eyebrows peaked. "Well I swear, Mariah, I've never heard you use such language. Calm down and let's talk about this home you keep referrin' to. You mention work? Where exactly do you think you work?"

"I don't *think*, I *know*." She lifted a defiant chin. "I'm an attorney for Fennster and Smith. I live in a three-bedroom townhouse with my husband, David Morgan. What else do you want to know?" She chewed on a ragged thumbnail, then glanced at her hands and frowned. "God, what happened to my manicure?"

Doc Samuel's brow arched as he cradled his chin between his thumb and forefinger. "An attorney, eh? My, my! This townhouse...is that a special kind of cabin or home?"

Taylor stood. "Oh c'mon! Everyone knows what a townhouse is." The shrillness in her voice reflected her frustration as she glared down at the pudgy little man. "Honestly, are you people living in the dark ages here? It's 2002. Get with the program."

Frank's eyes widened and his jaw dropped. "*What* year did you say?"

CHAPTER EIGHT

Denver, Colorado--2002

Mariah gasped. "It can't be! What do you mean 2002? It can't be, it just can't be."

David patted her shoulder. "Honey, calm down. What year do you think it is?"

"I don't want to calm down. Tell me you're joshing. It can't be 2002. I know it's May, but the year is 1872."

His eyes widened. "Taylor, you're scaring me. Tell *me* you're kidding!"

"I'm serious, and I really am Mariah. Why can't you understand that? It's 1872. I was born on March 7, 1837. If it was truly 2002, I would be long dead and buried."

"Tayl... Mariah. I don't even know what to call you." The color drained from his face. "Listen to what you're saying. There is no possible way that could be. Look at your hands and arms. Do you see the skin of someone over a hundred years old? Do I look like someone who lives in 1872? Look around you at all the modern conveniences. None of this existed in the 1870s."

He made sense and that frightened her. Her stomached knotted. All the things around her *were* strange, including him. Tears welled. "I know that, David, but I'm from 1872, and all this scares me to death. If I am really your wife, why are all the things I remember about another time, another life and another husband?"

David rubbed her hand. "I don't have an answer." He stared at the ceiling for a moment. "But I do have an idea. If you really are Mariah, then describe yourself to me."

"Why would you ask me to do that? You're looking right at me."

He shook his head. "No! I'm looking at Taylor Morgan."

Mariah exhaled in a long sigh. Would this nightmare ever end?

"Go ahead, Mariah... if that's your name. Describe yourself."

His mocking tone bothered her, but what would it hurt to describe herself? She decided to play along. "All right. I'm five feet, three inches tall. I have long red hair, green eyes, and a birthmark on my left shoulder."

He didn't speak, but stared at her and shook his head. "Wrong! You are totally wrong."

"How can I be? I certainly know what I look like."

David walked to the other side of the bed, removed the box of tissues and water glass from the tray table, and opened the top to reveal a mirror. He turned it toward her. "Look at yourself and tell me what you see."

Mariah's mouth gaped. There was some bruising on the face... but the eyes... the lips. She leaned closer and touched the cheek reflected in the mirror. She felt the touch, but it wasn't her face. A small bandage on her forehead didn't hide the fact that the hair she saw was not red like hers—it was brown with blonde streaks. Until recently, a huge dressing had hid most of it from her sight. As if willing the strange reflection to go away, she slammed the tabletop shut. "Oh, my God. Oh, my God," she groaned.

David reached around and untied the back of her

gown. Her modesty offended, she grabbed the neckline and held it tight. "What are you doing?" Panic tinged her voice.

"Don't worry. I only want to have a look at your left shoulder."

She relaxed her grasp on the gown and leaned forward, certain she was about to be vindicated, but her mind still whirring from what she'd seen.

He pulled the material down and inspected her shoulder.

"You see it, don't you? It's almost a perfect clover shape." She craned her neck, trying to see what she knew was there.

David shook his head and re-tied her gown. "Nope. No birthmark."

Mariah covered her face and broke into sobs. There had to be an explanation, but what? Whose face had she seen in the mirror? It certainly wasn't hers.

David perched on the bedside and took her in his arms. "Maybe I shouldn't have pushed you. Please don't cry, honey. We'll get you better, I promise."

He kissed the top of her head and rocked her back and forth until her tears ebbed. Finally, she relaxed in his embrace. An involuntary sigh escaped her lips. For the moment it didn't matter who he was; she needed his comforting.

He leaned her back against her pillows and wiped the glistening tears from her cheeks. "Honey, it's going to be all right. First you need to let your body heal, then we can get some professional help for you."

Mariah pulled the blanket up to her chin, rolled away from him and stared at the wall. She pondered his reference to professional help. What kind of help was that? Nothing made sense.

He patted her on the hip. "I'll run along so you can get some sleep."

Upon hearing the door open, she assumed he'd gone. She rolled over in time to see his face peeking back through the doorway. His eyes sparkled. "I forgot to tell you. The nurse said Doctor Shaw has cleared you to come home tomorrow. I'll be back around ten in the morning to pick you up. Sleep well, darling."

Mariah stared at the closed door through blurry eyes. She wondered if she had gone completely mad. She'd heard stories of people who'd lost their minds. Was this what they felt like? She wiped away her tears, sat up and reached for the rolling tray next to the bed. She'd watched the nurse open it before and place something inside. With a deep breath, she lifted the lid and exposed a mirror. Her gaze drifted to the foot of the bed and her heart pounded. How could she bear to look upon a face she didn't recognize a second time? She slammed the table top closed and kicked the metal stand away, then curled into a ball.

But the woman's image haunted her. Brown eyes and hair that shone like sunshine nested within the strands. What had happened to her long red tresses? And what of her birthmark? She'd had it her whole life. Frank often kidded her about being his lucky charm. She raked her knuckles across her forehead and moaned. She had to look again.

Her arm ached when she supported herself on it—the one that still bore a pierce mark surrounded by an ugly black circle. Her whole body still hurt when she moved… or was it her body. She didn't know anymore.

With a grimace, she pushed herself off the edge of the bed and nabbed the corner of the tray table. She pulled it closer, and supported herself against the mattress edge while steeling herself with courage. Her breath seized when she revealed the mirror again. She stooped for a closer look.

The eyes reflecting back at her blinked when she blinked. The lips moved when she opened her mouth, and she felt the fingers trailing along them. The hand belonged to the arm she moved, and the brow crinkled with the worry she felt. But who was this person? It wasn't Mariah Cassidy, she knew that for certain.

CHAPTER NINE

Colorado Territory—1872

"2002?" Frank stared wide eyed from his wife to the doctor and back again. "I don't know what to say. You're joshin', aren't you? You know its May 28, 1872, right?"

"*Right*," Taylor answered. "I'm your visitor from another dimension!" She pulled her mouth into a sneer. The man was a psycho.

"Mariah, and yes you are Mariah until you prove me wrong, I have no explanation for your strange behavior. I certainly can't understand why you believe you are in the year 2002." Frank's tone revealed his frustration. "I can't even imagine that far in the future, but I believe there would be some newfangled things invented by then. Don't you? Can't imagine how they could make things better than we have it here, but…" He spread his arms and indicated the decor as if it didn't look like a throwback to what she imagined her great grandmother's bedroom resembled.

Taylor pondered his ridiculous point. She glanced around the room. The patchwork quilt, the pitcher and wash bowl, his story about the horses and wagon, and the clothes hanging in the armoire—they certainly were relics from another time. She snapped her fingers. "I've got it. You operate a dude ranch where you try to replicate the Old West, right?"

Frank's shoulders slumped and he glanced at Doc

Samuels. "Doc, help me out here, would ya? Tell her."

"Mrs. Cassidy, Frank here speaks the truth. I—"

"No, I don't believe it. If I'm wrong, prove it to me."

Frank massaged the back of his neck, then stopped. His face brightened. "I've got it. You think someone dyed your hair red, don't you?"

She tugged on a lock and gave it a sideways glance. "Yes, and I hate it. That was a nasty thing to do to an injured person."

"What color eyes does Taylor have?"

"What a stupid question. Here I am. Have a look for yourself." She leaned forward and stretched her eyes as wide as they'd go.

"Fine, I will." He stood toe-to-toe with her. "Green. I see the same beautiful green eyes you've always had."

She stepped back and stared at him. "Green? Okay, besides being absolutely clueless, you are also colorblind. My eyes have always been brown." She crossed to the mirror and leaned in. The bruises around her eyes had diminished and the swelling had cleared. "See, I told y…you… Oh, my God, my eyes *are* green!"

She felt as though the air had been sucked from her lungs, and with no explanation, she sank onto the bed.

"What color eyes did you say you have?" Frank asked in a teasing tone.

Still denying what she'd seen in the mirror, Taylor gulped. She gazed up at Frank. "What's happening here? I know I have brown eyes."

She walked back to the mirror for verification, this time focusing on the entire face and not just the eyes. She gasped. Her head pounded. The room spun. She felt herself falling, then total blackness enveloped her.

* * * *

Taylor clutched at consciousness, sensing someone bathing her brow. "Ummm, where am I?" Afraid to open her eyes, she grabbed the air and locked onto an arm. "David, is that you?"

A sigh of disappointment sent warm breath across her face. "No, it's me, Frank. You fainted. Doc Samuels said there's nothing more he can do, so he's gone back to town. How are you feeling?"

She opened her eyes. Mariah's husband sat on the edge of the bed with a pan of water nearby. He removed the cloth from her head and dipped it into the liquid. After wringing it out, he spread the cool compress back across her brow. She blinked a few times.

Memories from their conversation flooded back and desperation returned. She flung the damp material from her forehead and sat up. "How am I feeling? *How* am I feeling? What do you think? I just saw a complete stranger in the mirror."

Silence ensued for a few minutes while Frank retrieved the compress and reimbursed it in the water. His eyes narrowed beneath the visible stress lines creasing his brow. "Mariah, I don't understand this anymore than you do. I wish we could just go back to the day it happened and start all over. The only thing I can tell you is that you look like my wife and you sound like my wife. Until I believe you aren't, I'm going to treat you like the Mariah I love."

Strangely touched by his genuine feelings for this Mariah person, whoever she was, Taylor softened. Stress drained from her rigid spine, and she sagged back against a pillow case damp from his ministrations. The tone is his voice convinced her he felt as baffled as she did. She gave a slow shake of her head. "I don't pretend to know how you feel. But I think we both agree this whole thing is confusing. Actually, it's just plain scary."

Taylor ran her hands through her hair. "Why is the face in the mirror not mine? And you're right. The eyes I see are green, the hair red, the lips wider, the skin paler. It's not me." She touched her bosom. "This is not my body! How can I be someone I'm not?"

The creases in Frank's brow deepened. He patted the back of her hand. "I don't know. I guess we can only take this a day at a time and see what happens. It appears we don't have much choice."

She nodded. "I guess you're right, but I have to say, so far things aren't going very well." She turned her lips down in an exaggerated pout.

Frank mimicked her facial expression then gave a half-hearted chuckle. "It hasn't been much better from where I sit either."

The tension between them drifted away and unanswered questions reeled through her mind. Two kept returning to the forefront: how did one find a way back to a different century and how did she know she Frank wasn't right about her being his wife? Even the doctor believed it to be true. The dilemma made her head hurt.

Frank's logic rang true. Maybe time would provide the proof she needed. In the meantime, there seemed no need to be a bitch.. She inched closer to Frank. "Well, if we're going to take it a day at a time, what do you have planned for tomorrow?"

CHAPTER TEN

Denver, Colorado—2002

Awake before the nurse came for what she called her morning rounds, Mariah lay in bed and stared at the ceiling, waiting for the usual prodding and poking. Rather than deal with worry, she clung to one positive thought. At least, today, she was finally getting out of bed.

She closed her eyes, pictured Frank and their children, and wished when she opened them, she'd be back home with her family. The doctor and nurse entered and interrupted her thoughts.

Doctor Shaw approached the bed, his smile broad. "Well, Mrs. Morgan, you get to go home today. I'm so pleased with your recovery, but I want you to take it easy for a couple of weeks. I wouldn't consider going back to your job right away, if I were you."

Job? Mariah glanced from the doctor to the grinning nurse and puzzled over the word. She massaged the furrow in her brow. Did he mean being lady of the ranch? That wasn't a job, but her responsibility. Warmth filled her when she pictured her bright kitchen and visualized cooking a wholesome meal for her family. She hoped upon hope to be returning to her comfy ranch home.

"But, what about my memory problem?" She almost laughed as soon as she'd asked the question. To her, everyone else had problems recalling the truth. She definitely knew who *she* was.

The doctor grasped his chin and appeared to ponder. "Well…physically, you've made rapid improvement, but I'm not sure about the memory issues. I'm hoping the loss is just a side-effect of the accident. But I suggest if you don't start getting things back into perspective soon, you might want to consider consulting a psychotherapist. If you like, I can recommend someone."

Psychotherapist? The word held no meaning for her. Accustomed to sighing of late, she released another and fought the flush creeping up her neck. Embarrassed at requiring constant explanations, she decided to wait and ask David about the suggestion. She smiled and nodded at the doctor. "Yes, that would be nice." Every time someone spoke, more confusion crept into her already befuddled mind.

The doctor scribbled something on a piece of paper and handed it to her. "Here, I'm sure you'll like her."

Mariah glanced at a name then lifted her chin, forcing a smile. "Thank you…and thank you for taking care of me, too." Even if he hadn't solved the puzzle about how she came to be here, he *had* tended her injuries and offered encouragement.

She put the paper on the side table then obediently stuck her arm out for the nurse. "I really won't miss having my arm squeezed every day." The simple statement came out more like a grumble.

* * * *

Mariah took the clothing the nurse gave her to the place everyone referred to as "the bathroom." It resembled the water closet Frank was building, but with more newfangled equipment. She touched one of the knobs on the basin, turned it, and took a step backwards when water spewed all over the place. Quickly, she stepped closer, turned the lever in the opposite direction then brushed droplets from her arm.

Her mind jumbled at all the strange new things she saw and heard around her. She focused her attention on the toilet, an intended addition to Frank's improvement. She'd seen one in a catalog. Truly amazing! No more trekking out to the privy or relieving oneself in a chamber pot kept under the bed.

She flushed the toilet and watched the water swirl around the bowl and disappear, then refill. Worry niggled at her. She took a deep breath, and tried to comprehend going "home" with a total stranger. Her options were limited. She had no idea where she was, how to find Frank, or even if he existed at all. Had she conjured him up in a dream? At least David seemed to care a great deal about her. Sometimes a little too much, in her opinion. An exhalation fluttered her lips as she convinced herself he really was a nice man and she had nothing to fear from him.

Mariah unfolded the clothing. Three pieces: A jacket, a blouse and another piece that didn't consist of much material. She hung the tops on the door hook then held out the mystery piece for examination, holding the short garment against her waist.

Surely this isn't the bottom.

It didn't even reach her knees.

Lordy, I can't wear this. It's indecent.

She re-folded the items, then pulled her hospital gown back around her and reached behind to make sure it was tightly tied. "Some of the doilies in my parlor cover more than these…these garments."

She left the bathroom and crawled back into bed.

David walked into her hospital room with a big smile on his face. "Hey! I came to take you home, Mrs. Morgan."

Behind him, the nurse entered, pushing a wheeled chair. Mariah'd heard about them, but this one had shiny wheels and handles. David bowed and gestured toward it. "Your chariot awaits, my lady."

Being called Mrs. Morgan no longer bothered her. There were far more important things to worry about. Until something happened to help her prove her real identity and explain all the craziness, she'd decided to stop fighting. Mariah eyed the chair's seat and back. If it had hand tooling, the leather could have been from one of Frank's saddles, and looked equally uncomfortable." Do I have to sit in *that*?"

"Yes, you do," the nurse answered. "It's hospital policy. Everyone leaves in a wheelchair."

David glanced at her with a raised brow. "Honey, why didn't you put on your clothes?"

"Ah...I'm still pretty sore," she lied, too embarrassed to admit her modesty. "I decided this is more comfortable. Is that all right?"

"Sure. We're only going home."

While the nurse gathered Mariah's few personal items and put them in a bag, David walked to the night table and picked up the piece of paper left behind by the doctor. "What's this?"

She fought to remember the long word Dr. Shaw used, but couldn't. "The doctor recommended some Pisco... pisco... something or other for me to see if my memory doesn't return."

"Psychotherapist?"

"Yes!" She bobbed a nod. "That's the word he used. Maybe I could pronounce it if I knew what it meant."

David laughed, but quickly sobered. "I'm not making fun of you. You sounded so cute and childlike, totally unlike yourself."

"So, what is a psycho… however you say it?"

"A psychotherapist is a different kind of doctor—someone who works with a person's mind."

"Then, I'm *not* going." She crossed her arms. "I'm perfectly happy with my mind the way it is. I'm not crazy! I don't have an explanation for all the strange things that are happening, but that doesn't mean I'm deranged."

David patted her shoulder. "Don't worry. Psychotherapists don't do anything *to* your mind. They listen, ask questions and analyze what's going on. It's quite painless and often very helpful. Come on, let's go home. We can talk about it later."

Mariah scrunched her mouth into a frown and slid off the bed.

"Fine, I'll go with you, but I absolutely refuse to have someone meddle with my mind."

What would it hurt? The question plagued her.

She made sure her gown was properly closed and dropped onto the wheeled chair's cold seat, she clucked her tongue against her teeth. "Well, I might consider it, but I'm not making any promises."

CHAPTER ELEVEN

Colorado Territory—1872

Taylor stared up at the ceiling.

God, there's nothing to do around here.

She considered getting out of bed, but lacked motivation. Glancing across the room at the mirror, she squelched the need to throw something at it—break it so she couldn't be reminded every day that she *was* Mariah Cassidy. She twirled a lock of red hair around her finger, pondering the mystery surrounding her.

How could she explain feeling like Taylor Morgan but looking like Mariah Cassidy? Could she fathom being stuck forever in Mariah's home, with her children and her husband… her so very handsome husband? The last thought struck a guilty note. David was just as handsome, and somewhat used to her cursing.

Noticing she played with her hair, Taylor unwound the strands from her finger and pulled the lock straight out in front of her face. "Damn, I hate red hair!"

At a light tap on the door, she inched higher against the headboard. "Come in," she called out.

Frank entered, filling the room with the scent of fresh soap and leather. "Good morning. I wondered if you wanted to come down to breakfast."

Taylor shrugged. "Well, I guess I should eat something even though I don't have much of an appetite."

"Maybe a change of scenery will help. I'd like to take you on a tour of the Rocking C afterwards. That is if you feel up to it." He stuffed his hands into his pockets.

She thought a moment. Getting out of the house and into fresh air might do her some good.

She slid off the bed and stood. "That sounds great. I'll get dressed and be right down."

Almost out the door, Frank glanced over his shoulder. "You know, Mar... I'm sorry, Taylor. I don't know if I can ever get used to this. You're Mariah in my eyes. But, we'll work through this somehow. I just don't want you to be upset anymore."

Taylor fought a sudden urge to reach out and push a stray lock of dark hair away from his eyes, but instead clasped her hands together at her waist. Frank looked so innocent and scared, she forced a smile. "I know. This is hard on both of us. I guess we only can take a day at a time. None of this makes any sense at all. I keep feeling like it's a strange dream that's going to end any minute."

"Well, before you wake up, come on down and eat some breakfast, then we'll go for a ride."

His good nature lightened her mood.

* * * *

Taylor found her appetite as soon as she spied the biscuits and gravy. She took a seat at the table and hungrily split open two big flaky rolls and smothered them with creamy gravy. Seeing heat vapor rising, she carefully took her first bite. After she swallowed, she paused before a second taste. "Yum! My compliments to the chef, whoever that might be."

Frank refilled his coffee cup then pulled out a chair

across from her. He turned it around and straddled it. Leaning against the back, he flashed a dazzling smile. "That would be me, I reckon."

"Well, you certainly are a good cook." She wiped the edges of her mouth with her napkin and took another bite.

"So are you... or you used to be."

Taylor wiped a gravy drip from her chin and burst into laugher. "There's even more proof I'm not who you think I am. I can burn water."

The silence deafened her. She glanced around. "Where are the children?"

"I had my foreman take them to my mother's house this morning. I figured it would be a little easier for everyone if the they spent a few days away."

Her mouth turned to cotton. "Frank, I'm so sorry. I didn't mean to run the kids away from their own home."

"Kids? Oh, you mean the younguns." He blinked away his confused look. "It's not your fault. Hell, I don't even know whose it is. Let me tell you, I've played this over in my head a thousand times since you woke up. I've tried being mad at Jacob for having to pee. I've tried being mad at the rattlesnakes. And I've definitely been mad at you a few times."

Taylor chuckled. "I can imagine. David says I'm not the easiest person to live with."

A lump formed in her throat. Mentioning her husband reminded her how much she missed him.

Frank took the last sip of his coffee and stood. "How about I get the buggy and pick you up out front? I had Lloyd bring it back when he dropped off the...*kids*."

She pushed her melancholy thoughts aside. "You've got a deal."

He flashed a boyish grin and removed his cowboy hat

from the rack next to the back door. Placing his hat at a jaunty angle, he stepped onto the porch. Taylor scurried to the counter with her dirty plate and peered out the window. Frank paused for a moment, unbuckled his belt and tucked his denim shirt in more snugly. She released a long, slow breath.

As if sensing she watched, he turned around and caught her gaze. She lowered her eyes and backed away from the window, too late to avoid his subtle smile and the flush creeping up her neck. Why did she feel like a child caught opening a Christmas package?

Unable to resist another peek, she waited a moment then leaned her head over just enough to see out. Frank ambled across the yard and into the barn. Damn, he was a good-looking man; there was no doubt about that. His blue jeans hugged an ass tight enough to bounce a quarter off, and shirt sleeves rolled up to his elbows gave him a rugged look. With the black hat as a finishing touch, she considered him very, very sexy.

"Girl, you have a husband at home," she chastised herself. "Stop slobbering over someone else's man. You're thinking thoughts you ought not be thinking, Taylor Morgan."

She turned somber again.

Did she really have a husband at home, or was she making up a whole other life?

* * * *

Taylor inspected the quaint little carriage. "So, this is the buggy we're riding in," she said with trepidation.

"Yep." He leapt down and came around to her side.

"And… this is your horse!" She cautiously approached the animal and stood close until its eerie stare made her shiver.

"I don't think he likes me. He's looking at me like I'm dinner."

Frank's Adam's apple bobbed when he threw his head back and laughed. "Don't worry, ol' Gert wouldn't hurt a fly. *She's* the best trotter I've got."

Taylor stared at the yellow, spoked wheels. "What's the difference between a buggy and a wagon?"

"A wagon is much sturdier." He patted Gert's muzzle. "The wagon would have been my first choice for the rough ground around the ranch, but I haven't gotten it fixed since…" His voice faded into a whisper until he cleared his throat. "I should have replaced the wagon wheel by now, but I've been distracted by other things."

"I wouldn't be one of those other things, would I?" she cooed, holding her head in a coquettish tilt.

CHAPTER TWELVE

Denver, Colorado—2002

With the nurse following, David wheeled Mariah into the hallway. She held steadfast to the arms of the chair and glanced down the long corridor stretching in front of her. The ceiling lights reflected in the highly polished floors and sparkled like a nighttime sky. As David pushed her along, she peeked inside each open door. She wanted to ask questions, but the answers to previous ones only made her more confused.

David maneuvered her chair around the corner, toward two large doors. He stopped in front and pushed a button on the wall. She sat silently, wondering what would happen. When nothing did, she glanced up at him. "What's the button for?"

"The elevator." He responded like she should know.

"Elevator?"

"Yes!" The annoyance in his voice smacked her like a slap in the face. "It carries people from floor to floor—we're going down."

Although puzzled by his attitude, she was more interested in this new-fangled lift. How did someone get carried from floor to floor by it?

The massive doors slid open to reveal a strange little room. Without a word, David turned the wheeled chair around and, tugging at its resistance to a raised threshold, bumped her up, over, and inside. After the nurse entered, he pushed another button, and the doors came together and sealed them inside. The metal prison sucked every bit of air from Mariah's chest. She panted in quick gasps, detesting the feeling of confinement in such a small area. David seemed unaffected and obviously didn't notice her state of panic.

She struggled to regain control of her breathing and composed herself. The movement stopped with a thud, but her stomach didn't. She swallowed the bitter taste of bile and took a deep breath when the doors opened. No longer afraid of using up all the air inside the cramped quarters, she exhaled and willed her body to relax.

When she focused beyond the doors, Mariah gaped in awe. Before her was not the long corridor, but a large, open, airy room busy with people. David pushed her out into their midst and she tightened her grip on the armrests of her chair. Small and unobtrusive, she sat while people passed all around her. Her head whipped from side-to-side, taking in the wonder of the different styles of dress, hair, and skin color.

Her eyes fixed on one certain woman. She wore something very similar to the scant piece of material the nurse had provided as clothing. She couldn't believe her eyes.

"Oh my goodness. That *was* the bottom part," she whispered, aghast at so much exposed skin.

Mariah's gaze dropped to the shoes the woman wore.

Father in heaven, she thought. How did someone walk on toothpicks.

She vaguely heard David say something about leaving the wheeled chair at the front desk, and looked up only long enough to wave as the nurse walked away. Her attention snapped right back to the amazing sights.

Beyond the crowd, Mariah noticed another bustling

world of people outside huge windows. Her heart raced as so many of the colorful vehicles David called 'cars,' whizzed by. They looked quite different from this angle--moved by themselves, without horses or mules.

She looked up at David and put her hand to her bosom. "Do we have a car?"

"Yes, we do. We had two before your accident. The Lexus was totaled, but thank goodness we have good insurance."

"Lexus? Insurance? He might as well speak in gibberish.

He clenched and unclenched his lips. "I keep forgetting you don't remember things. Lexus is the kind of car you had. Don't you recall? You loved driving it so much."

Mariah lowered her head. "No, I'm sorry. I don't have any recollections of a car. I can tell by the tone in your voice you're tired of me asking so many questions, but try to imagine what it feels like to be in my place. I don't remember *any* of this and it scares me to death."

"I'm so sorry. I should be more considerate." He put his hand on her shoulder. "I want so badly for you to remember." His fingers clamped into her skin as his remorseful tone turned urgent. "I want you back the way you were."

She understood his distress, but had no idea of his meaning. She'd always been Mariah and she liked herself... but in the place and time she remembered.

Her life couldn't be only a dream. Every part of it was etched in her memory--Frank, the kids, the ranch—how could she make it all up?

She looked at David through teary eyes. "I'm trying. That's all I can say for now. I'm trying. Please be patient a little longer."

He bent and brushed her lips with his. "I know you are . I am, too. We have to give it more time."

Startled by his spontaneous kiss, Mariah pressed back in the chair. Before he attempted another, she turned her head and stared out the window.

Kisses? Definitely not, but time? She could give him that. In fact, time was about the only thing she had left.

He steered her chair to a counter and stopped. She glanced up at him. "What now?"

"You sit tight and I'll go get the car." He pulled keys from his pocket. "I'll park in the loading zone and come get you."

At the thought of being left alone amidst strangers and riding in a strange conveyance to who knew where, Mariah's heart rate quickened. "I'll be right here," she responded with a bravery she didn't feel. Besides, where else could she go?

She drew her bottom lip between her teeth, worrying about what was yet to come.

* * * *

David wheeled her outside into the brightness. Despite the sun peeking through the tall buildings, the air felt crisp and cool. David's narration got lost in the loud din of the city—a city of which she'd never seen the likes.

He pushed the wheelchair toward a shiny, black *car*, and after pushing the brake lever on her chair forward, helped her stand. "Here we are. Let me get the door."

Mariah held her hospital gown closed, bent, and peered inside.

Her eyes widened at a big round wheel, levers on the floor—more strange gadgets. "God, please help me," she whispered.

A shiver of apprehension quivered through her as she sat on the seat's edge, turned and put her feet inside. David leaned in, stretched a belt across her body and locked it into a coupling of some sort. "I'll be right back," he said, and closed the door, sealing her inside. She prepared for the same feeling she'd experienced in the new-fangled elevator, but the surrounding windows provided a much more open feel.

Afraid to move, she scanned the interior further. She touched the soft material overhead with one hand, while her other one caressed the seat cushion. She splayed her fingers against the cold glass window, then eyed the meters and knobs before her. How could someone forget such things?

David interrupted her inspection when he slid in beside her. "Are you ready?"

"I suppose." Her heart pounded, partly in anticipation and partly from fear. He pulled his own belt across his lap and locked it, then inserted a key into a slot and turned it. The conveyance came alive. The hair on the back of her neck bristled and she jumped. "What's that noise?"

"Don't be scared, it's just the engine." His laughter began to annoy her. She saw nothing funny in her logical questions.

"Is it supposed to sound like that?"

"Yes, dear, all cars sound this way. I just had ours tuned. Remember?"

Remember, remember. Is that all you can say? If I remembered, would I ask? I'm going crazy. I don't remember, I don't, I don't, I don't.

Using both hands, she pushed her hair behind her ears and forced herself to be calm. "No, but it's not important." She blew a silent blast of air through pursed lips. Cars, Lexus, tuned: too much to consider.

David's foot applied pressure to a lever on the floor. He looked over his shoulder and pushed harder, and they surged forward into the line of other cars. Mariah held her breath and grasped the side of the seat. She forced herself to keep her eyes focused straight ahead as they approached the car in front of them.

The ride wasn't as scary as she'd expected, in fact, a lot smoother than a wagon, and David appeared to know what he was doing. Despite wondering how they moved so fast, she sagged into the seatback, loosened her grip and relaxed.

From the corner of her eye, the scenery outside seemed to move instead of the car. Her stomach rolled, and she felt ill. The feeling lessened if she looked directly through the front window. She focused on the road ahead.

The landscape changed the farther they traveled. Houses rather than tall buildings now lined the streets. Beautiful homes decorated with shrubs and grass. She always thought her home beautiful, but these were very different. She looked from one side to the other, not wanting to miss a thing.

The car slowed before houses situated so close together, they reminded her of the buildings around the mercantile. David turned into an opening in front of a brick building and stopped. "We're home," he announced with a grin.

She stiffened at his announcement.

His was a two-story, just like her home on the Rocking C but larger. David got out, came around ad opened her door. She stood, clutching her hospital gown, and stared wide-eyed at the sea of green, evenly cut and separated by a brick walkway that matched the house.

David looked at her. "If I'd known you weren't going to wear your clothes home, I would have brought your robe.

Let's get you inside." He led her past a door labeled 1A.

He stopped at 1B, inserted a key, pushed open the door and stepped inside. With a bow, he made a sweeping gesture. "Here we are. Welcome home."

Shouldn't she remember this? Her mind reeled. Cars, houses of all colors and sizes, buildings taller than the hills around the Rocking C. Her hard swallow pushed down the lump that formed in her throat.

She reached out and touched the plaque on the door. "What does 1A and 1B mean?"

David's lips thinned. "Those are the address numbers of the condos. There are two together. Next door is 1C and 1D and so on."

Condos? She wasn't asking. She'd just assume condo was a new word for home.

A shiny, marble floor greeted her in the entryway. She touched the small blossoms on the wall covering, then took two steps and sunk into a downy rug, the largest she'd ever seen. It wasn't even braided and went from one wall to the other.

She looked at David. "This…this is breathtaking." She didn't know what else to say. The room was full of beautiful things—furniture, paintings, plants.

Could they really be hers? How could she forget such lovely things?

CHAPTER THIRTEEN

Colorado Territory—1872

Frank, already seated in the buggy, took Taylor's hand and helped her inside. She tried to manage a graceful entrance, but the hem of Mariah's long dress caught on the carriage step and Taylor nearly fell backwards. She flailed her arms and struggled to retain her balance, grabbing Frank's hand in her panic. "Geez Louise, how in the hell do women maneuver in these things?"

He clasped her hand and steadied her. "Careful!"

Taylor plopped next to him, pulled her full skirt inside and tucked it under her legs. Once settled, she smoothed the material and folded her hands in her lap. "Okay, give it the gas, I'm ready!"

He tilted his head and gave her a sidelong glance. "I'm not even gonna ask your meaning. No doubt your answer'll be just as confusin'." Frank rippled the reins and the buggy began to roll. Gert's slow pace was consistent with her age.

Taylor leaned back and relaxed. She'd never taken a horse and buggy ride before, and she inhaled a deep breath of fresh air. It felt good to be out of the house. Besides an occasional birdcall, only the slight creak of turning wheels and the clip-clop of Gert's hoofs on the hard dirt disturbed the morning stillness.

A beautiful day loomed. Taylor straightened to view the breathtaking scenery. For endless miles, expansive fields of swaying grass and wild flowers colored the landscape. The sun, inching toward wisps of white clouds floating high in a powder blue sky, created the perfect backdrop. A cool morning breeze caressed her face, and her body moved in sync with the swaying buggy. For the first time in days, she found herself enjoying something.

Frank hadn't uttered a word since they passed under the big C on the front gate. He leaned forward, arms resting on his knees, and held the reins in both hands. He stared straight ahead, seemingly lost in thought. Since the brim of his hat partially hid his face, she had difficulty determining his mood.

He'd talk eventually, she felt sure. He started the day in a good mood and she hadn't done anything to ruin it.

Craning her neck to see beyond the crest of the next hill, Taylor's breath hitched. "Oh, this is beautiful. I've never seen such a serene setting. Is all this land yours?"

As if her cheerful statement woke him, Frank leaned back and pushed his hat off his forehead. "Yep, this is all *ours*."

For a fleeting moment, Taylor's hackles spiked at his inference they were a couple, but she took a big gulp of fresh air and decided to ignore it. Her gaze roamed from side-to-side, her eyes widened. "It's really beautiful. I've never seen such vibrant colors. How did you...we come to own so much property?"

He made a clicking nose to urge Gert up a small knoll. "My father started the ranch years ago, but it got to be too much for him. I'm an only son, so he passed it on to me."

"Where does your family live now?"

Frank's jaw tensed. "My father died a few years back."

Taylor rested her hand atop his. "I'm sorry for your loss. I can't imagine losing a parent. Mine are very dear to me." Her heart ached at the thought of never seeing her own again.

She dismissed her worry and focused on Frank. "What about your mother?"

"I still have Ma." The sparkle returned to his voice. "She shares a home with my spinster sister. We'll have to pay them a visit."

"Great," Taylor mumbled far beneath her breath. The last thing she needed was more strange faces spouting memories of which she had no recollections. She simply smiled and nodded.

Frank stopped the buggy in a little valley and turned to Taylor. "Let's get out. There's something I want you to see."

He jumped down and went around to her side of the carriage. Spanning her waist with his long fingers, he lifted her as if she weighed nothing and placed her on the ground. With his palm in the small of her back, he urged her toward the top of the hill. At the crest, he pointed. "What do you think?"

The sea of grass had become fodder for a huge herd of cattle. For as far as she could see, cows dotted the landscape. Taylor's mouth gaped. "I've never seen so many animals in one place." She shielded her eyes from the sun with her hand and scanned the area. "Oh, Frank, it really is beautiful here."

He smiled and draped his arm around her shoulder. "Does it jog any memories for you?"

She shook her head. "I'm sorry. It doesn't. But that doesn't make it any less spectacular. This is breathtaking."

Uncomfortable with his show of affection, she took a step forward and bent to pick a wildflower. She held it to her nose and inhaled the faint sweetness. "Thank you for bringing me here. I've truly enjoyed the outing. I never would have guessed your ranch was this big."

"Ours!" he corrected.

"All right, *ours*," she relented. "I know what you're hoping for, but it's not going to work. I wish I could be Mariah for you… I can't. I may look like her, but I'm Taylor and nothing is going to convince me otherwise."

Frank's stony gaze pierced her. He grabbed her upper arms and pulled her close. "I'll never believe that you aren't Mariah."

He searched her face. His probing eyes mirrored the desperation she'd just heard in his voice. She tensed at his sudden change of mood and struggled to get free. "Let me go!"

Instead, he tightened his hold and crushed her against him. "You feel so familiar… so good."

Before she could object, he bent his head and boldly covered her mouth with a searing kiss.

Taylor's conscience screamed for her to stop, but her body argued. The feel of lips against hers stirred familiar sensations—ones she missed. He pulled her closer and trailed his hand along her back. Goosebumps peppered her arms; her nostrils filled with his manly scent. Blinded by need, she snaked her arms around his neck and leaned into him, pushing her mouth harder against his.

He's not David. Stop! Her conscience argued with her needs.

Her husband's name echoing in her mind brought her to her senses. She shoved Frank away, keeping him at arms' length. "Stop, please. We mustn't."

He took a deep breath and stepped back. "You seemed to enjoy it. What's wrong?"

She gazed into his probing blue eyes. "Don't misinterpret what just happened. I shouldn't have responded the way I did. It's not right. I'm married to someone else. I got caught up in the heat of the moment."

Frank adjusted his pant leg. "I'll say it was a heated moment, and it felt good. No, damn it—it felt wonderful! I've missed your kisses. I've missed holding you in my arms and making love to you. It's not right to expect a man to go so long without lovin'. You always welcomed my kisses and—"

"No! Mariah welcomed your kisses and shows of affection. I'm not her, remember?"

Frank shook his head. His lips pulled into a frown. "No, I don't remember. I look at you standing before me and I see Mariah. I kissed you and tasted Mariah. How in God's name do you expect me to think of you as anyone else?" His shoulders sagged.

"I think we should go back to the ranch now. I don't want to talk about this anymore." Taylor abruptly turned and walked back toward the buggy, but glanced over her shoulder to see if he followed.

He took his hat off and slapped it against his leg. "Fine! Maybe you aren't Mariah after all. She never ran from a fight and always faced problems head on. I'm beginning to wonder if I'm really who I think I am." He stomped down the hill, silently helped her to her seat, then took his own. Gert stepped lively at Frank's hefty flick of the reins.

The ride back to the ranch was a quiet one. Taylor kept her head turned from him so he couldn't see the tears of frustration running down her cheeks. Poor Gert was forced to endure a much faster pace, as it appeared Frank was eager to have the outing come to an end.

CHAPTER FOURTEEN

Denver, Colorado—2002

David led Mariah to the bedroom and had her stand in front of two wide doors. "This is your closet." He opened it and stood aside. "Find something comfortable to put on. You must be tired of holding that gown closed."

Mariah stared at the clothing inside. She slid the colorful hangers apart and inspected each garment. Her armoire paled in comparison to the array of pants, dresses, shirts, and skirts she viewed. Even a few things she couldn't identify as clothing.

She fingered a see-through piece of silk adorned with fluffs of fur. Her eyes widened and she glanced at David but dared not ask where someone wore such a flimsy piece. "Someone certainly has a bounty of things."

"Taylor, it's your closet."

"*Mariah*," she corrected him. "And it's not *my* closet. I've never worn anything like this before." She thrust a pair of blue jeans toward him.

"Just try them on. You wear them all the time." He reached up to the overhead shelf, pulled down a red shirt and handed to her. "Here, put this on with them. You like wearing jeans and a tee shirt."

She held up the top and wrinkled her nose. "It just doesn't seem proper."

"Trust me. You'll like wearing them once they're on.

It'll be better than the gown, I promise. He put his hand on the door knob. "I'll leave you to change." He left but the door re-opened slightly and he peered inside. "By the way, your underwear is in the top left drawer of the dresser."

Alone in the room, Mariah clutched the clothing and looked around. Her gaze rested on the bed, with its huge headboard and ornate posts. A whole family could sleep in it.

She looked across the room, at a dresser covered with multi-colored bottles and jars.

Mariah laid the clothes atop the bed, walked over, and picked up one of the many different vessels. She wrestled with the top and jumped when a fine mist dampened the side of her face. A sweet aroma filled the air.

The squinted at the writing on the bottle's bottom, but the print was far too small to read. *Must be toilet water. Sure smells good.*

She turned the opening toward her neck and sprayed behind her ear, then examined the tiny pinhole in the cap. "Lordy, what will they think of next?" For good measure, she sent another spritz wafting in the air.

Mariah put the bottle back where she'd found it then inspected the others. With her curiosity satisfied she opened the designated underwear drawer. Her mouth gaped at the contents, and she held up a scant piece of material by two fingers. She eyed the other items and sneered. How could this possibly be an undergarment? They looked nothing like her comfortable chemise. There were no camisoles or corsets, just bottoms and things she assumed were tops… and those didn't look very comfortable. Only the bottoms even compared to a chemise. She held one up for closer inspection, trying to decide which, if any, to wear.

Well, I can't possibly wear these. Part of them appears to be missing.

She dug through the entire pile before she finally found and selected the closest thing to plain, white cotton drawers. Turning her attention to the strange breast covers, she held one up against her chest to see how it looked.

Now all she had to do was figure out how to put it on. What she wouldn't give for her comfortable, one-piece chemise. She'd even settle for her corset.

She fumbled with the contraption until she figured out how to hook it.

Since the accident, she'd been without undergarments. It seemed strange to wear something so confining. She inspected herself in the mirror, turning around to look from every angle, then touched her breasts and smiled at her reflection. She didn't look so bad, although her chest was a bit bigger than she was used to, but….

She reluctantly donned the clothing David had selected and looked at her reflection again. Although the pants felt strange and the shapeless shirt had the word 'NOW' imprinted across the front, she had to agree with him—they were much more comfortable than the drafty hospital gown.

* * * *

Mariah walked through the house, looking at and touching the walls, the window coverings, and the fabric on the furniture. The flowers on the table looked real but she discovered they weren't when she bent to smell them. She flexed the fake petals and clucked her tongue against her teeth. "Seems nothing is real here."

David appeared from the hallway. "What do you mean?"

"Fake flowers, see-through unmentionables, these things called tee-shirts." She yanked at the material and smiled. She bent down and splayed her fingers through the lush carpeting. "Even rugs that cover every bit of the floor. David, your home is perfect."

"*Our* home," he corrected.

Mariah shuddered and stood. She wrung her clasped hands. "No, this isn't my home. You can't make me be someone I'm not. I have a whole history in my head that doesn't fit any place in this time period. I don't know what's true or not anymore, but I do know being Mariah Cassidy seems very right."

David dropped into a big leather chair and peered up at her, despair in his eyes. "I'm trying not to rush you. I just keep praying you'll remember who you are and where you're from." He leaned back and pushed against the arms—a footrest popped up.

Mariah gaped. "How did you do that?"

"Do what?"

"With the chair?" She bent to look underneath.

"It's called a recliner." He chuckled and pushed the weight of his body against the chair back and stretched out even further.

Mariah furrowed her brow and shook her head. "Lordy, I couldn't forget all these wondrous things." She crossed to the sofa and perched on its edge. "Is this going to do anything strange?"

David displayed perfectly straight teeth in a wide smile. "No, you're safe. This is the only reclining piece of furniture we own."

Mariah wanted to see more; in fact she wanted to see everything in this place David called her home. She sprang to her feet. "Would you mind if I looked through the rest of the house?"

He kicked himself back into a sitting position and stood. "Of course not. Let me show you around."

David led her into a bright, cheery room. Her eyes widened as she took in all the strange sights.

This looks like a kitchen. That thing over there could be the stove. That's definitely a basin of some sort. Oh, but what's that big boxy thing next to the stove? Where are the table and chairs?

"This is our kitchen," he said, confirming her suspicions. "Come to think about it, this room probably won't jog any memories for you." He chuckled. "You don't believe in spending much time in here. I don't mean to hurt your feelings, but we both know you aren't a very good cook."

"Oh, is that so?" She squared her shoulders and held her head high. "I believe you're wrong about that. What would you like me to prepare for you?"

"Yeah, right." David snickered. "Hmm, let's see." He grasped his chin, seeming to give her offer thought. "I know! I've been craving pot roast."

"That's easy enough. Do you have all the fixin's?"

"Besides the meat, what else do you need?"

"Potatoes, carrots and onions." She ran the ingredients through her mind and rattled them off. "Do you have those?"

"Carrots and onions in the refrigerator, potatoes under the counter, but I'll have to run to the market to buy a roast. I tried to stock up on some things, but I guess I forgot meat. I'm not used to someone cooking around here."

She didn't understand what he found so amusing, but while he laughed, she scanned the kitchen.

Which of these things could be a refrigerator?

Luckily, David walked over and opened the door of the big box. Inside were shelves and drawers, and lots of containers. David bent over and slid out one of the drawers to retrieve the fresh vegetables.

Mariah craned her neck to see around him. "Oh, you meant the ice box. Goodness, this one even has a light inside." She viewed the contents and pointed. What's that?"

David held six cans bound by see-through material. "It's *Pepsi...* soda." He tore one from its binding and thrust it behind his back. "Would you like one?"

"Yes, I believe I would. I'm thirsty." She surveyed the colorful container. "Does it taste good?"

He pulled his head out of the refrigerator, took the can and popped a piece of metal on top. "Here, have a taste."

Mariah took the can and sniffed the contents. It had little smell. She tipped the can to her mouth and took a big gulp, then immediately pinched her nostrils together. "How very strange. Little bubbles tickled my nose and now I feel like they're inside me. Is it supposed to feel like that?"

He grinned. "Yes, it's called carbonation."

She tipped the can again and took another drink. "Well, I certainly like carbon--"

Before she could finish the word, she belched loudly. She muffled a giggle and felt her cheeks warm. "Oh, I'm so sorry. Excuse me."

"That's a side effect. It happens to most of us." David's eyes sparkled, making Mariah uncomfortable beneath his gaze.

She put the can down on the counter and turned her attention back to supper. "Well, show me where the pans are and I'll get started. Where did you say you're going to get the meat?"

"The supermarket a few blocks away."

I'm not even going to ask if that's a fancy word for the mercantile.

She worried about being left alone for the first time, but squared her shoulders in false bravery. "Please hurry back... and before you go, please show me where the knives are so I can cut up the vegetables."

He pulled out a drawer full of different sizes of carving knives. "Here, take your pick." Then, in rapid motion, he pointed out where things were located. "If you need bowls, they're up in that cabinet. If you need dishes or glasses, they're in that one and the pans are inside the doors next to the stove. I'll be right back with the roast."

As soon as the door closed behind him, Mariah roamed around the kitchen, opening doors and drawers. Her mind raced at the marvels that filled them. She fingered the intricate "M" etched into the drinking glasses, and jumped back in fright when the contraption hanging under the cabinet came to life when she pushed its handle.

Another question hung on her lips to ask when David returned, but now she needed to find a pot. She opened the cupboard he'd indicated.

Lordy, I've never seen so many pots and pans. How could a body use so many?

It took quite her awhile to decide which one to use.

She moved to the refrigerator and eyed it with apprehension. Then, taking a step back, she grasped the handle and gave it a tug. The door partially opened. Mariah peeked around it, expecting something to jump out at her. When she felt certain nothing would, she opened the door fully and rifled through the contents—milk, eggs, jelly, jam, a packet of ham slices. She slid the bottom drawers in and out, gaping at all the food.

Heavens, it's like having a mercantile in your own home.

She opened the smaller door on top. Icy air escaped and caressed her cheeks when she took a step closer to peer inside. She touched one of a few wrapped packages—hard as a rock and very cold. She licked off the snow-like piece of ice clinging to her finger and closed the door. It seemed every gadget was more wonderful than the one before it. This all had to be a dream and she was bound to wake up and share a good laugh with Frank. She pinched herself and felt pain. "Okay, so it will take more than that to wake me. I'll be patient."

Mariah moved to the big basin, grasped the handle and moved it to the right. Immediately water poured out and sent a fine spray splashing upward. Although she'd had a similar experience at the hospital, with the glee of a child, she clapped her hands each time she turned it off, on, and off again. "Imagine, a cool, clean drink whenever you want."

A lever-like device protruding from the wall caught her attention. She reached over and flipped it up. Immediately the basin growled at her. With a trembling hand, she pushed the lever back to its original position and stepped away. She quivered at the thought of touching anything else, stood in the middle of the room, and turned in a slow circle.

"Surely, the vegetables won't grumble at me." She moved to the counter to prepare the ones she needed. While chewing her bottom lip, she prayed the basin didn't growl at her again, and cautiously approached to clean the potatoes.

How can I possibly explain all of these things? Oh Frank, if only you could be here to see the wonder of this place… or dream.

CHAPTER FIFTEEN

Colorado Territory—1872

Taylor lay curled atop the patchwork quilt and tried to make sense of things. She pulled her knees up and wrapped her arms around them, finding comfort in a fetal position. The sunset bathed the bedroom orange and yellow. Hours had passed since Frank dropped her off at the front porch and disappeared into the barn. Not wanting to face him, she sought shelter in the bedroom, but secretly hoped he'd come looking for her. The clock downstairs chimed to announce the half-hour and her head spun with a million thoughts.

Is this ever going to end? Am I really Mariah, and David is just a figment of my imagination?

Guilt tugged at her heart.

Why did I let Frank kiss me? Why did I want him to kiss me?

She heard footsteps coming up the stairs and waited to see if he knocked. Instead, the door across the hall opened then closed. Taylor took a deep breath, got up and lit the lamp. How she missed flipping a switch. She moved to the window and pushed the curtain aside. Only the sun's tip was visible, and shadows of the barn stretched across the yard. Through the burlap covering the bunkhouse window across the way, Taylor watched shadows pass.

Her stomach rumbled, reminding her she hadn't eaten in hours. She tiptoed to the door and opened it enough to peer out. Frank's door remained closed so she sneaked down the stairs and, into the kitchen.

In the pantry, she smeared butters over a slice of bread and poured herself a glass of milk. She took a drink and shuddered. "It tastes horrible when it's warm," she muttered. "How in hell does anyone stand this stuff?"

She poured it back into the pitcher and popped the last bite of bread into her mouth.

Taylor stole back up stairs, reaching the top just as Frank opened his door. The firm set of his jaw hinted he was still annoyed. "Oh, you're awake." The flat tone of his voice confirmed it.

Taylor fidgeted beneath his stare. "I got hungry. I went down and had some bread and butter."

Barefoot, he walked into the hallway and stood in front of her. His unbuttoned shirt revealed a chest well-muscled and tanned. Her eyes rested on the fur-carpeted area between his nipples, then trailed down the thin line of hair that disappeared beyond his waistband. Taylor's cheeks burned.

Stop looking at him like that. He'll get the wrong idea.

She feigned a yawn and stretched her arms over her head. "I'm still tired. I think I'll go back to bed."

He stepped into her path. "Wait a minute. We need to talk."

"Frank, please. What else is there to say? I can't explain what's going on and neither can you. I think I'm crazy."

His warm breath pelted her face.

She tried to go around him, but he grabbed her arm. "You're not crazy. At least I don't think so. But I know what you mean. I'm beginning to wonder about my own sanity." He ran his fingers through his curly, black hair. "Do you have any idea what it's like for me? I lay in bed across the hall, knowing you're only a few feet away. My body aches for you, Mariah. I need to hold you." His beguiling eyes seared her very soul. "Please, just let me hold you. I don't care what you think your name is."

Taylor broke eye contact. Not knowing how to respond, she took a deep breath and willed the right words to come. Her skin burned beneath his fingers and her body grew uncomfortably aware of his closeness. Finally, she looked at him and said, "What do you want me to say? Do you want me to lie and tell you I'm Mariah?"

Frank let go of her arm and stared at the floor. "No, I don't want you to lie to me. I just thought..."

"You thought what?" She knew she shouldn't

ask.

"I thought if I could hold you in my arms, you might come back to me."

Taylor pondered his words—her rationale impaired by needing intimacy. His nearness, his clean male scent, and the stray lock of hair on his forehead all conspired against logic.

What can it hurt? Maybe something will change. There can't be anything wrong with just lying in his arms for a while.

"Okay," she blurted, before her sense of reason returned. "I don't want to feel this way anymore. I think I need to be held."

She took his hand, led him into her bedroom and paused to shorten the wick on the lantern.

Reality crept in. She stood with her back to him, in awkward silence, and stared at the bed. He stood so close. His heat, his inhalations... something snapped inside her.

What the hell am I doing? Making a big mistake, that's what.

The woman inside her argued.

No, it's not a mistake. It's okay. You're just going to hold each other.

Frank twirled her around and unfastened two buttons on her dress before she jerked away. "What are you doing?"

"I didn't think you'd want to sleep in your dress."

Her flesh tingled against the roughness of his

hands. She dropped her arms to her sides. "You're right, I don't." Despite her words, her mind made a last-ditch effort.

Stop, Taylor! Stop it now or...

He fumbled with the last button. Goose bumps rose on her exposed skin. He tugged the top of her dress down to her waist and inched it past her hips. It fell to the floor and lay in a heap around her feet, leaving her shivering in an old-fashioned chemise. He reached and pulled the quilt back so she could get under the covers.

Lying on her side, she nervously clutched the quilt to her chest and watched as he removed his shirt. The veins in his well-muscled biceps bulged ever so slightly when he flexed his fingers to unbuckle his pants. Part of her wanted to admire his naked form but guilt made her close her eyes. His buckle clanked against the floor when he dropped his pants. She opened one eye barely enough to see him clad in a knee-length cotton undergarment—not so different from David's boxer briefs.

The thought of her husband chilled her. What would he think if he knew? But did he exist? Common sense and intelligence ruled out anything she conjured up in explanation. Right now, she needed passion. She needed to know *she* was real.

Frank blew out the light on the table. The bed dipped beneath his weight.

She shivered, turned over and backed up

against him. He draped an arm over her and pulled her close. His skin felt cool next to hers.

A clear image of David's face flashed in her mind and she froze. *Taylor, what are you thinking? This isn't right. You should stop!*

But Frank's breath warmed the back of her neck and his arm tightened around her. "Mariah," he murmured.

Taylor was sick and tired of bickering about names. Somehow, at the moment, it didn't seem important. "Yes," she answered softly.

He rolled her over and peered into her eyes. "I need you."

Did he see her or his wife lurking in the depths? She wanted to ask, but he snaked an arm beneath her and pulled her into an embrace. After he tucked her hair behind her ear, he warmed her exposed lobe with a breath. "Just let me hold you."

Her breath hitched in her throat and her toes curled.

She forced herself to relax and mold against him. All thoughts of wrongdoing evaporated from her mind. "Yes, please hold me... hold me tight," she whispered back.

Frank buried his face in the hollow of her neck. His lips trailed along her collarbone and sent shivers coursing through her. He covered her neck and shoulder with kisses and gently nipped at her flesh.

She wanted more.

With a deaf ear turned to her good conscience, she arched her back and offered him access to her bodice. She trembled as his fingers clumsily tugged at the ribbon of her chemise. With it finally untied, he pulled the material off her shoulder and exposed one breast. He gently kneaded her nipple between his thumb and forefinger. His breathing grew rapid.

His teeth captured her hardened nipple and gently tugged. "Oh, yes... yes," Taylor moaned. His hand moved to free her other breast.

She wove her fingers through his hair and pulled his head closer. His erection pushed hard against her, and she knew she should stop, but couldn't. She wrapped a leg around his hip and boldly pushed against his maleness.

Stop it. It's going to be too late. Stop it now.

Suddenly, he rolled her onto her back and rose to his knees above her. She froze in place as he tugged her chemise down around her ankles and finally completely off.

He paused for a moment. His gaze raked the length of her naked body then locked on her face. "Tell me you don't want me to stop." His guttural words were more a plea than a statement.

"Don't stop," she heard herself whisper. "Please, don't stop now."

Frank straddled her. She touched his hardened member, ran her hand up and down the length of it. He groaned low in his throat and leaned forward to again suckle her breast. She encouraged his full erection while he explored her innermost part with his fingers. She writhed beneath him, and spread her legs to allow him full access, craving penetration.

His mouth abandoned her breast and traveled slowly down her body, stopping to lap at her navel with his tongue. When she moaned in ecstasy, he buried his head between her thighs.

His ministrations drove her to frenzy. She held his head against her crotch, encouraging him to continue his feast. His tongue darted in and out, lapping at her pulsing nub until his sensual expertise sent her over the edge. "Yes, Yes, Yes!"

Taylor's hand reached for his manhood and guided it toward the juncture of her thighs. She pressed his member against her pubic hair, now wet from his oral caresses. Whimpering, she arched her back against him and called out his name. "David, oh David…" She stiffened.

Her faux pas went unnoticed, but her heart filled with remorse. Again, she asked herself why, as she lay limp beneath a man who so dearly loved the woman he believed her to be. Was he right?

"Mariah, my darling Mariah. Let me love you. Does that feel good? Do you like that?"

She did. Not only liked but needed to be loved. Regardless of where she belonged, for the moment she was here. She forced thoughts of everything but Frank from her mind. "Yes, oh yes. It feels good… so good,

Frank. For tonight, I'll be your Mariah."

CHAPTER SIXTEEN

Denver, Colorado—2002

Mariah had the potatoes and carrots chopped and ready when David returned. He handed her a package wrapped in white paper. She placed it on the counter, opened it and found the most beautiful piece of meat inside. She turned and smiled. "This should cook up very nicely. It'll take a few hours so I hope you work up an appetite between now and then. I'm going to show you what a good cook can really do."

"Oh really?" He raised a brow. "Based on previous experience, I have serious doubts. Up until now you haven't been at all interested in cooking."

"You certainly can't be talking about me. I've always loved to cook and I'm good at it."

"I suppose I should be thankful for your newfound culinary interests, but until I sample dinner, I'll just be thankful we have canned soup in the cupboard."

She crossed her arms and scowled. "We won't be needing that. Just you wait; you'll sing a different tune when supper is ready."

He grinned. "Okay, I'll go warm up my vocal cords while I watch some TV. Call me when it's time to eat."

Mariah chuckled. "A few days ago, I didn't even know what a TV was. "

* * * *

Mariah gave David's shoulder a gentle shake. He awoke with a start. "I... I didn't realize I had dozed off." He took a deep breath. "What is that tantalizing aroma?"

"Dinner," she said smugly and walked back into the kitchen.

She stood at the counter dishing up the pot roast when arms snaked around her waist and David nuzzled her neck. "Smells wonderful, baby," he purred.

Mariah gasped, and quickly turned and pushed him away with her free hand. Holding the carving knife in the other, she glared at him.

David held both hands up in the air. "Whoa! I'm sorry. It's a habit. I'm sorry if I offended you."

She lowered the knife and sighed. "I don't feel offended. You startled me. I know you believe I'm Taylor, but in my mind, I'm not! You're not Frank and he's the only man who can touch me in such a personal way."

David nodded. "I'm sorry. It won't happen again—at least until you're ready."

"And, what makes you think I'll ever be ready?" She glared at him, unable to fathom he still didn't believe her.

"Oh, c'mon, Taylor. Eventually, you're bound to remember who you are. I need to give you time and I'm willing to do that. So don't worry about me forcing myself on you."

Mariah took a deep breath. "Thank you. I truly hope that some of this starts to make sense very soon. But you may well be the one in for a shock."

David plucked a piece of meat from the plate and tasted it. He licked his fingers and cast a boyish grin. "Well, I never would have gotten so personal if you hadn't fixed such a delicious roast."

His remark lightened her mood.

* * * *

David tossed his napkin on his empty plate, leaned back in his chair and rubbed his stomach. "That was delicious."

Mariah stood to clear the table. "And you said I couldn't cook."

"Before the accident, believe me, you couldn't... or wouldn't. Actually, I'm not sure which."

"Like I said, I've always liked to cook," she called over her shoulder as she carried dirty dishes to the sink. "My mother taught me at a very early age. Frank thinks I'm the best cook around."

"Frank again! Always Frank!" David's voice boomed.

Mariah shuddered at his sudden change of attitude, but his tone of voice mellowed as he walked into the kitchen. "Well, whoever he is, I have to agree with him. You *are* a great cook."

She turned on the water to fill the sink.

David came over, turned off the tap and picked up the dirty dishes. "Here, let's put these in the dishwasher."

"Dishwasher?" She shrugged her shoulders.

He lowered the front of the machine, pulled out a rack and placed the dishes, silverware and dirty pot in slots and pushed them all inside. From the door beneath the basin, he removed a box of powder which he poured into a receptacle in the door. He put the machine back together and turned a dial.

The immediate whirring sound surprised her. "This washes the dishes?"

Curious as to what went on inside, she bent and put

her ear to the dishwasher door. She straightened and asked, "What happens if I open it?"

David grinned. "Honey, I can't believe how clueless you've become about so many things. Sometimes it's really annoying and sometimes it's just downright cute."

She ignored his remark. "So, what will happen?"

"Okay, Miss Curious. It will stop until you close it again." David wandered into the living room leaving her to ponder yet another miracle.

"My heaven's, what will they think of next? Cars, televisions, dishwashers..." She hung the dishtowel on the sink and followed him. A resounding 'thunk' drew her attention back to the kitchen. She took a step backwards and glanced from side to side, but saw nothing. "David," she called out, "I heard a very loud noise in here. It sounded like something falling."

He peeked around the bathroom door. "Check the freezer. I'm sure it's only the icemaker."

Mariah drew back, her mouth agape. "Icemaker?" she mumbled. "I don't even want to know."

CHAPTER SEVENTEEN

Colorado Territory—1872

Taylor opened her eyes. Recollections of last night flooded her mind. She remained perfectly still and cast a sidelong glance to see if Frank still lay beside her. The bed was empty. She rolled over and pulled the extra pillow to her chest. His heady scent lingered. Evidence thrown about the room proved it hadn't been a dream. Her chemise hung haphazardly on the water pitcher and, on the floor, her dress still crumpled on the floor where she'd stepped out it.

She crushed the pillow to her face.

Taylor, Taylor how could you? Why?

But she knew why—loneliness. Her breasts still tingled from his caress, and she remembered distinctly his kisses mapping a trail across her body. His lovemaking rivaled David's in every way, but that didn't ease her mind. She sighed and rolled to the other side of the bed.

Get up, Taylor. You have to face him sometime.

She plucked her chemise from the pitcher and sat on the bed. The memory of his calloused hands, so different to David's soft white palms, jerking the fragile ribbons of her chemise loose haunted her, taunted her. She shook her head to chase away the vivid images, walked to the armoire and tried to decide which of the horrendous dresses to wear today.

God, I can't believe these are my choices. Where's a Macys when you need one?

* * * *

In the barn, Frank held three long nails between his teeth and fought to keep the mare's hoof still. His mind wasn't on his work—maybe that was the problem. Visions of Mariah, crushed beneath him in their downy feather bed, rolled through his mind. Last night was perfect. Hell, it was better than perfect. Never had she responded with such…such passion.

He brought the hammer crashing down on his thumb. "Hell's bells!" He clenched his teeth. "Pay attention or you'll nail your hand to a hoof."

When he finished shoeing the mare, he slapped her on the rump and sent her trotting back into the corral. He washed his hands in the water bucket then wiped them on his pants. Movement caught his attention and he glanced toward the house. Mariah sat on the porch, a coffee cup in her hand. He ambled in her direction, hoping last night had spurred her memory. The experience had certainly stirred something within him. Doubts niggled at him.

He stepped up and removed his hat. Holding the brim with one hand, he ran the other through his matted hair and cleared his throat. "Good morning, pretty lady. Did you sleep well?"

Her head jerked around. A blush colored her neck and blossomed onto her cheeks. "Ah…quite well, thank you." Her neck quivered with a hard swallow. "We need to talk. Care to join me?"

Frank plopped down in the other rocker and crossed his legs. He placed his hat on the table between them. "Whadda we need to talk about?"

She took a deep breath. "About last night... it can't happen again."

Disappointment stabbed at his heart. "Why not? I thought you enjoyed it. I know I did."

"It was wonderful, but that's not the point. I still believe I'm married to someone else and I don't care to feel like a cheating slut."

Frank shook his head. "I'm sorry if last night made you feel cheap. That certainly wasn't my intent. I thought I'd given you enough time, but evidently I was wrong. I'll try to respect your wishes."

She crushed her knuckles to her lip then lowered them. "You aren't the cause of my feelings. I'm punishing myself. You didn't force yourself on me. Honestly, I needed you. I've always been a sexual being... I drive David crazy. But, like I said, let's chalk it up to a mistake and know it *won't* happen again."

Frank stood, picked up his hat and slapped it against his leg. A flurry of dust sifted through the air. He stared down at her. "You can call it a mistake if you want, but it wasn't for me. I've made love to you a thousand times, and last night was one of the most memorable. You've never been so willing and free with your body. Nothing that wonderful could be wrong."

He stomped back to the barn and began mucking the stalls. His neck muscles corded and his jaw ached from clenching his teeth since his discussion with Mariah. With a sigh, he stopped shoveling, wiped the sweat from his brow on his shirtsleeve then leaned on the spade handle. The stench of manure hung heavy in the air.

What a turn his life had taken. His wife had changed in so many ways since the accident. Although she looked the same, he wondered if maybe she *was* somebody else. Thoughts of last night kept flashing through his mind. It was Mariah's body he made love to, but she'd never reacted with such passion and wanton lust. She always acted the proper lady, even in bed. Last night was definitely different. He shook the silly notions from his head, threw down the shovel and filled his arms with fresh straw.

* * * *

Taylor watched him swagger across the yard. The man had a sexy walk. She took a deep breath and fought her building desire for him and tipped her coffee to her lips. It'd gone cold. She set the cup on the table and pulled her legs up under her. Resting her chin on her hand, she pondered how long she could be strong.

It won't happen again, Taylor... it won't.

She rose and went into the house, wandering through the rooms, snooping through drawers and cupboards. Nothing struck a familiar chord. Being in limbo grew tiresome. She walked into the parlor and perched on the edge of the settee. Before, she'd only stood in the doorway, but now she sat with hands primly folded in her lap and scanned the room, hoping something would jump out at her. The quaint furnishings and handmade doilies gave the room a homey feel. Lovely though it was, her shoulders sagged. There was nothing in the room that smacked of her personality in the least.

She glanced at the picture above the fireplace. Mariah's face—her own face—stared down at her. Moving to the hearth for a closer look, she leaned on the wooden mantel, rested her chin on her hands and stared up at the portrait. She sensed absolutely no connection, even when she closed her eyes and searched her memory.

When she opened her eyes, she noticed the imprints

her hands and elbows left in the dust on the wood. It occurred to her the house was in dire need of a good cleaning.

I haven't made a move to clean anything since my accident. If I'm going to be the lady of the house, and it looks like everyone but me believes I am, I'd better get busy.

She went into the pantry and found a flour sack. The printing on it had long ago faded and the material had grown soft, most likely from countless washings. On the way back to the parlor, she realized there was probably a pile of dirty laundry somewhere. She shook her head. It could wait. She had no interest in mimicking the old westerns she'd seen and spend time stooping over a washboard. It was hard enough for her to believe she suddenly found dusting an interesting pastime.

Without the thick layer of silt, the dark mahogany tables shone brightly. She wiped away her prints from the mantel and straightened the pillows on the settee. Amazingly, she enjoyed herself, even hummed a cheerful tune.

* * * *

She knelt on hands and knees, washing the floor when Frank came inside. He stopped dead in his tracks. "Whoops! Guess I'd better not track up what you've just washed."

An unpleasant odor hung on him like a fog and his boots bore evidence of mucking the stalls. He backed out the door, removed them and left them outside, then stood in the doorway in his stocking feet. "Is it dry enough for me to come in?"

Taylor struggled to get up. "Damn long dresses," she murmured under her breath, surprised that Frank didn't seem angry anymore. She wiped her brow and smiled. "Yes, it should be dry over there."

He tiptoed across the floor, into the dining room. "I'm getting hungry. How about you? I haven't had anything since breakfast."

Taylor's stomach growled at the mention of food. "I haven't had anything but coffee. I sure would like something."

She felt a slight pang of guilt that Frank had done all the cooking, but she eyed the big, old stove with curled lip. She had no idea how to cook on something so archaic, and besides, she abhorred kitchen chores.

CHAPTER EIGHTEEN

Denver, Colorado—2002

Mariah never knew something as marvelous as a shower existed. She stood under the pelting spray until the warm water turned cold, then dried off with a downy bath towel. Even the large 'M' displayed on the material felt soft against her skin. She stood in her bathrobe and flushed the toilet for a second time, still amazed at how the water swirled around the bowl and disappeared.

A person could really get used to all these modern conveniences.

She turned on the tap to brush her teeth, and glancing in the mirror, pondered the strange image staring back at her.

Why do I believe so strongly this isn't my face? Where did I go? Could I be wrong? Am I really Taylor Morgan?

She ran her fingers through unfamiliar thick hair and tucked it behind her ears. She sighed as she put away her toothpaste and brush, closed the wall cabinet, and took one last glimpse of her reflection.

It isn't really such a bad one.

The miracle she hoped for was slow in coming. The dream she kept waiting to awaken from lingered on and on. Frank couldn't possibly be a product of her imagination. She missed him too much for him not to be real. But how did she make David believe her?

As she came out of the bathroom, she collided with him in the hallway. He wore a white robe matching hers. She averted her gaze from his bare chest. "Oh, I'm sorry. I guess I should watch where I'm going."

"No problem. I was on my way to take a swim. Want to join me?"

"Swim? Where?"

"We have a pool in the backyard, remember?"

Mariah hadn't ventured that far yet. "We have a swimmin' hole?"

He chuckled. "Where did this new language come from? I said pool... swimming pool."

Her cheeks heated. The fact he found her speech so different only proved she wasn't the same person. And was a pool the same thing as a hole?

David took her hand and led her to the curtained wall in the living room. He pulled on a piece of hanging cord and the material parted in the middle, revealing a huge window. Beyond was a large fenced area filled with plants, flowers and an expanse of green, all next to a large pond of crystal blue water.

She could barely wait for him to open the door. Once outside, she strolled from one end of the yard to the other, smelling the flowers and walking barefoot in the lush grass. She paused at the edge of the pool, knelt and wiggled her fingers in the water, then gazed up at David. "I've never seen anything like this in my life." The phrase rang all too familiar. Her days were filled with strange new things she'd never even imagined.

David took off his bathrobe and dove in, drenching her with the resulting splash. He surfaced, rolled over on his back and kicked his feet. "You always had your heart set on having your own pool. You were on the swim team in college, and you love water. Logical match. Go get your suit on and join me."

Mariah wiped the back of her hand across her dripping face and pushed back a soggy strand of hair. She crinkled her nose at the strange almost medicinal smell hanging in the air. "What suit?"

She averted her eyes from the flimsy bit of material that clung to his evident manhood.

"Swimsuit. You have twenty-five of them at last count." He chuckled.

"I don't know how to swim... at least I don't think I do." Her head ached from trying to remember.

"Taylor," his voice turned stern, "believe me, you're a swimmer. Go change. Once you get in the water, it will come back to you. It's like riding a bicycle."

"Bicycle?"

He rolled his eyes. "Never mind." He waved her away. "We'll talk about that later. Just go get changed. This will be good therapy for your sore muscles."

She cringed at having to ask yet another question. "Where would I find my swimming clothes?"

"Bottom drawer, right hand side, I believe."

She went inside, rummaged through the bottom drawer and pulled out tops and bottoms resembling pieces in the undergarment drawer. "Heavens," she mumbled. "I can't possibly wear anything so revealing—especially in front of David."

But, he expected her to join him.

Mariah tried on a few, but shed them quickly when she glanced in the mirror and saw how much flesh she exposed. Finally, at the drawer's bottom, she found a single piece that covered more than any of the others. She put it on and turned in a full circle in front of the looking glass.

At least this one doesn't display every part of me... but I still feel naked as a jay bird. I can't go out there like this.

David called to her. She snatched the robe from the bed, wrapped it around her and stepped outside. "Here I am." She ignored her thudding heart.

"Well, don't just stand there. Take that thing off and come on in. The water's warm."

Mariah stood clutching her wrapper with white knuckles. David paddled to the shallow end and extended a hand. "C'mon. Just stand on the stairs until you're ready."

She dangled her foot over the side and tested the water, then stepped down. "Oh, it does feel nice."

Mariah braved the second step.

"Take off your robe," he said a second time. "You're gonna get it wet."

"I… I don't know if I can. I'm not used to… exposing so much of myself."

"Look, Taylor. I've seen everything you have. You're my wife. I've made love to your body a thousand times." He waded closer and cupped his hand to his mouth. "This may come as a shock to you, but I've actually seen you naked."

His words lit a fire that flamed her face. She lowered her eyes and fought the urge to argue. Her mind formed words she wanted to scream at him.

You have not seen me naked. You may have seen Taylor, but not me.

"Really," David continued to prod, "come on in. You'll enjoy it."

She had no way out. With a deep breath, she flung the robe onto a nearby chair, scampered into the shallow water, and crouched beneath the surface until nothing showed but her neck and head. The water felt surprisingly warm. "All right, I'm in. Are you satisfied?"

Hopefully, she hadn't revealed too much.

* * * *

After several futile attempts to move beyond the shallow end, and sinking like a rock, Mariah wondered why David still insisted she was a swimmer. Tired of gagging and choking on swallowed water, she'd reached her boiling point. Her jaw ached from tensing it.

She pushed saturated hair out of her face and glared at him. "See? Are you convinced? I do *not* know how to swim. You may find this fun, but I certainly don't."

With anger bubbling, she realized she stood in shallow water, bearing her body to him. It didn't deter her. Her concern over modesty had shifted to surviving the swimming pool.

"I'm sorry, honey. I thought you'd enjoy it." He covered his mouth.

Is he laughing at me?

When she caught a glimpse of her reflection in the window, she understood. Rivulets of water dribbled down her face from hair askew and plastered strangely on one side of her head.

The sight only served to make her madder. "I don't know what you think is so funny. I'm getting out."

Scampering up the pool stairs, she grabbed her robe, threw it around her shoulders then flounced into the house. The sliding door slammed hard enough to shimmy the huge panes of glass.

* * * *

Despite David's apology, Mariah sat on the sofa with her back to him.

"I don't know why you're so mad at me. I only laughed because you looked so adorable." He touched her shoulder.

The sincerity in his voice caused her icy anger to melt. She turned to look at him. "I don't like people making fun of me. It seems you're either annoyed with me or laughing at something I've done. I thought it was kind of me to even try your silly swimming hole… pool."

He inched closer, his empty gaze focused beyond her. "I can't for the life of me understand how someone forgets how to swim. In college, you were Olympic-caliber." A sigh escaped him. He swiped his hand across his mouth, then smiled at her. "But, you were a good sport and I'm sorry I laughed at you. It won't happen again, I promise.

Mariah relaxed, letting the rigidity leave her shoulders. "All right, but next time I tell you I can't do something, promise you'll believe me."

"I promise!" He put his hand over his heart. "Hey, tell you what. To make up, how about I take you to a movie?"

Her smile sagged to a frown.

Oh, not again. You say something and I have to ask the meaning. I'm sick of this.

"Before you have to ask, a movie is like television only bigger, louder and with hot buttery popcorn."

Mariah licked her lips. It'd been a long time since she'd had popcorn and then only once. "I'd love to go. Should I change clothes?" She gestured toward the jeans and t-shirt she wore.

"What you have on is fine. Let me check the newspaper and find out what's playing."

Bigger and louder than television... and popcorn? She released a long breath. *As long as there is no water involved, I'm ready to give it a try.*

CHAPTER NINETEEN

Colorado Territory—1872

Frank looked down at his dirty clothes and stained hands. "Well, before I fix us something to eat, I think I'd better take a bath. After mucking the stalls, I'm sure you don't want to sit down to dinner with me smellin' like this. Usually one of the hands takes care of that chore, but they're tending cattle today."

Bath?

She couldn't believe her ears. "You have a tub? I've been using a pitcher and bowl to wash up everyday. You mean I could actually have been taking a *bath* instead?"

"You really have forgotten most everything, haven't you? The door next to the guest room hides my project in the works. Don't you remember... I'm building a water closet... like those newfangled ones in the catalog? We keep the tub in there. I don't suppose you recall when we went into town to order it?" His eyelids fluttered. "We still have to haul the water upstairs, but someday, I may even be able to connect it to the pump outside."

A relaxing Jacuzzi popped into Taylor's mind. "Okay, if it's 1872 and we don't have running water, how come I remember sitting in a huge bathtub with jets and massager? Why do I even know what they are?"

Frank's eyes reflected that familiar confusion she'd seen so often; he offered no response.

Something was very wrong with this picture. Had she been kidnapped and a ransom demanded? She dispelled the thought. A kidnapper probably wouldn't draw her bath and make her dinner.

With no explanation of her mysterious flashback, she dared not try to explain it, but she certainly wasn't passing on a real bath. "Lead the way."

Frank grinned. "Judging from the smile on your face, I guess I should have mentioned the tub sooner. You go on up. I'll put some water on the stove to heat."

* * * *

Thoughts of dinner dimmed as she watched Frank empty the first bucket of steaming water into the footed enamel tub. Her tired body yearned for a relaxing bath, but like everything else, Taylor compared the antiquated fixture to the modern conveniences she yearned for. *Oh, for a hot water heater and running water.*

The sound of Frank adding the second bucket interrupted her thoughts. She watched the rising steam. "I guess I should wait a minute or so until it cools a little."

"Unless you want to *be* dinner, that's a good idea." He closed the door behind him, his laughter fading as he descended the stairs.

Taylor stepped out of her clothing and dipped one foot into the water. It felt hot, but the longer she wiggled her toes, the more comfortable and inviting it became. She stepped in, sat and leaned back, sliding her body down into the shallow water. Her breasts were barely covered and her toes stuck out at the other end.

"Gee, another bucket or two would have been nice,

but..." she mumbled. *Stop griping, Taylor! Just enjoy the moment. It's better than the pitcher and bowl routine.*

She reached to a side table, picked up a bar of soap and rubbed it between her wet hands. A luxurious fragrance of lavender rose from the bubbles. The warmth already faded from the water, so she quickly washed then held her nose and submerged her head. After working the soap into a thick lather, she spread the foam through her hair, and dipped again for a quick rinse. Wincing at the soap sting, she knuckled water from her eyes and heaved a sigh. *I can't believe I just washed my hair in the same water I bathed in, **and** with hand soap. God, I miss my Paul Mitchell shampoo.*

She submerged one last time, hoping to remove the last traces of soap. Her hair was as clean as it was going to get, so she stood, and with water drizzling down her face, grabbed the towel hanging nearby.

"Crap!" She hadn't remembered to bring clean clothing.

Taylor wrapped herself in the towel, opened the door and started to dash across the hall. To her surprise, Frank leaned against the wall next to her door. He held a clean towel and his change of clothes. "Jes' waitin' my turn."

"Uh... excuse me," she said, her cheeks burning. She ran inside, closed the door, leaned against it, and took a deep breath.

Dumb, dumb, dumb. Taylor, if you don't want to get yourself into a compromising position again, you'd better plan a little better.

She shook her head to dispel the images of Frank undressing for his bath and searched the armoire. She'd grown tired of wearing the same dress but in a different print and looked for something else. What she wouldn't give for her jeans and a t-shirt.

She stopped sifting through hangers and tilted her head to listen. From across the hall, she heard Frank, and giggled at his slightly off-key baritone voice. Did he realize how loudly he sang? His serenade lasted only a short time before she heard a door close and footsteps padding across the landing.

Taylor winkled her nose at the thought that he'd bathed in her leftover water but turned her attention back to Mariah's armoire. There wasn't much variety, but Taylor finally decided on a burgundy skirt and a grey linen blouse rather than a dress. She elected to forgo the uncomfortable petticoats. If Frank's jeans fit her, she would have asked to borrow a pair. She chuckled at the imagined look on his face. His darling Mariah in something as outrageous as jeans?

Her stomach growled. It had been hours since she ate. Frank had finished his bath. She hoped he'd started dinner.

* * * *

Taylor took a final bite of fried potatoes and licked grease from her lips. She pushed away her empty plate. Surely, her stomach would object later, as she always steered clear of fatty foods, but right now she felt satisfied. "That was delicious. Thank you." She leaned back in her chair and smiled.

Frank rubbed his stomach. "Yep, it sure hit the spot. Dishes can wait till mornin'. I'm about ready to turn in. You?"

Recalling last night, she stiffened. "I-I think I'll sit on the porch and enjoy the evening air for a bit. If you don't mind."

"Mind?" His eyes widened. "Why should I mind? Go ahead, enjoy yourself. I'll see you in the morning."

He left her sitting at the table and disappeared up the

stairs. Her gaze fell to the dirty plates and utensils. *Okay, Taylor, he cooked, you can clean.*

She went out to the pump and returned with a filled bucket, but too lazy to heat the water, she washed the dishes in cold, dried and put them away. On her way back outside, she hung the damp dishtowel on the hook next to the door.

The melodic chirping of crickets filled the night, but stilled when the door slammed. The sudden silence sent a shiver through her and made her want to retreat back inside. The lantern light shining through the kitchen window provided enough illumination to calm her, and she sat and pulled her feet up under her. Leaning on her elbow, she gazed up at the stars and wondered about David. *Where are you tonight? Do you miss me?*

She heaved a sigh. Was he even real or someone she created in her injured mind? Her own mind questioned the things she'd argued so strongly with Frank.

Across the yard, the light in the bunkhouse faded to dark. The crickets began their serenade once again. Taylor's thoughts drifted to her previous night. Her skin warmed as she vividly relived Frank's caresses. The image only served to stir up guilt. With a shake of her head, she attempted to clear her mind, but it didn't help. Her attraction for him grew with each passing minute and it scared her.

She stood, walked to the railing, plucked a honeysuckle blossom and held it to her nose. Conflicted thoughts about her true identity buzzed through her mind.

Oh, Frank. Why are things still so hazy? If I am Mariah, why can't I remember how much I love you? And why is David the one who seems to own my heart?

Taylor let the petals fall from her hand and went back inside. Carrying the lantern, she quietly ascended the stairs. She paused, with her hand on the doorknob, and tried one last time to sort things out. Perhaps, when she woke... *Oh give it up, Taylor! Nothing is going to change. Maybe you should just accept the fact you are Mariah Cassidy.*

CHAPTER TWENTY

Denver, Colorado—2002

Mariah sat in the darkened theater, eyes fixed on the large screen. She tried to follow the movie, *Insomnia,* David had selected as their evening's entertainment. He seemed excited because someone named Al Pacino had the starring role. As she watched in awe, loud gunfire reverberated throughout the theater. She jumped.

Al Pacino, peering through a heavy fog, realized someone had shot his partner. Bathed in the emotion of the moment, a tear slipped down Mariah's cheek, and she brushed it away, wondering why she cried for people she didn't even know. She reached into her bucket of buttered popcorn, tossed a handful into her mouth and followed it with a big drink of soda. Her eyes never left the screen until it went dark and the lights came up.

Mariah blinked several times to adjust to the sudden change. Everyone around them rose to leave, but David stretched his hands over his head, arched his back and yawned. He glanced over her. "So, what'd you think?"

"I'm not sure. I know you explained movies to me in the car, but this seemed so real, I cried."

"Then I guess it was a good show. It's supposed to make you feel what the characters feel."

He stood. "I'm beat, are you ready to go?"

Mariah wiped the greasy sheen from her fingers. "I'm ready." She finished the popcorn then slurped down the last of her soda. David took the empty containers from her and led her down the darkened hallway into the lobby.

On the quiet ride home, her thoughts turned to Frank. What would he have thought about the movie? About everything?

Oh Frank, I miss you so. What are you doing right now? Do you miss me?

Before she realized they were home, David pulled into the garage and pushed the button to close the door. Still amazed by all the wondrous gadgets, she wondered how he could believe she had forgotten so many things. Her life, as she recalled, was very real and she remembered every aspect it. It didn't include any of these amazing contraptions like dishwashers, machines that opened doors, and a magic box that held a never-ending supply of little blocks of ice.

Always the gentleman, David hurried around to open her door. Taking her hand, he helped her out of the car. "I hope you had a good time tonight, Taylor. I know I did."

Mariah stood on her tiptoes and placed a perfunctory kiss on his cheek. How many times did she have to remind him who she was? "*Mariah* had a very nice time, David. Thank you. The movie was quite entertaining."

He followed quickly on her heels as she entered the house. "The evening doesn't have to end here, you know? It's still early."

She turned to see him adjusting his pants. "What do you mean?" Trepidation quivered her voice as she eyed a noticeable bulge.

"I need to hold you, to make love to you. I know I promised I wouldn't rush you, but haven't I waited long enough?"

"I'm very tired, David."

A look of disappointment crept into his eyes. She almost wanted to apologize.

* * * *

While getting undressed for bed, Mariah's stomach began to cramp. Had she eaten too much popcorn? Knowing she couldn't yet sleep, she put her robe on and went to join David. He lay stretched out in his recliner watching TV. She started to take her usual place on the couch, but the pains worsened. She excused herself to go to the bathroom.

She lowered her pants and sat on the toilet. Blood spotted her underwear. She rolled her eyes. *Oh, my gosh, I've started my monthly. Why now, oh Lord? I wonder where the rags are kept.* Until she found them, she folded some toilet tissue and placed it in her panties.

With the uncomfortable paper between her legs, she waddled back into the den and stood between David and the TV. Her cheeks turned to fire. "I've…I've started my monthly time. I can't remember where we keep the rags."

"Rags?" He kicked his recliner into a sitting position, one brow peaked.

She stared at the floor. "Yes, you know, the ones f-for this time of the month."

He rose and went into the bathroom. She followed and watched while he knelt and searched under the sink. He pulled out a box, and handed it to her. "Here, I think this is what you need. Honestly, Taylor, have you forgotten everything? And where in the world did that reference to *rags* come from?"

"It's all I've ever used." She scanned the label on the carton. "Super absorbent Tampax?" She sighed, pulled one from the box and stared at it while rolling the cylindrical tube in her hand.. She looked at him and shrugged. "What am I supposed to do with this?"

David's jaw tensed. "They're tampons. Don't tell me you don't even remember how to use them?"

"I have no idea. I can't even guess from looking at one."

David took the tampon and pulled it apart. "It's not like I know from experience, but you put the whole thing inside you. This part comes out." He held up the outer shell in one hand and a strange piece of cotton with a string attached in the other. "You leave this part inside to absorb the…blo…flow. You know it isn't easy to teach someone something I know nothing about." A flush crept up his neck and colored his cheeks.

She pondered his directions and winkled her nose. The thought of inserting something inside herself repulsed her. "I think I prefer to use a rag, if you don't mind."

David snatched the box from her and shoved the tampon back inside. He stooped down to search again. "Aha, I think I found something you can use."

He handed her another box.

"Wings?" She took the box and read the label. Reaching inside, she pulled out a cotton pad and turned it over in her hand to examine it. "This does look a little more like what I had in mind." She held it up. "But what are these things on the side for?"

He expelled an exasperated breath. "I'm not sure." He grabbed the box and read the directions. "It says you fold them around the sides of your underwear to give you greater protection." He handed them back to her. "These are things I prefer not to know."

"And things I'd prefer not to discuss." Her cheeks

flamed again. She'd never discussed such personal things with Frank—never considered it. She meekly thanked David for his help, placed her hand in the middle of his back and pushed him out the door.

Mariah leaned against the wall and took a deep breath, clutching the box of strange pads. Tears burned the back of her eyes. How could she have forgotten so much? No matter how hard she tried, she couldn't make sense of anything at the moment.

CHAPTER TWENTY-ONE

Colorado Territory—1872

Sleep eluded Taylor. She tossed and turned while thoughts of David filled her mind. The image of his face seemed so real. If she really was Mariah Cassidy, then why did she remember every detail about him? The tattoo on his left shoulder, his firm behind, the way he kissed and caressed her — everything was vividly etched in her mind. She couldn't be wrong.

Frank seemed a kind and decent man, but he wasn't David. Before she drifted off, she prayed, as she had so many times of late. *Oh God, please tell me David is real and I'm not imagining him.*

It seemed she had just fallen asleep when she heard a ruckus outside the window. She pushed the curtain aside and peered out to see several wagons in the yard. Each carried two or three women. Watching as Frank helped each of them down, she counted eight in all. She had no idea who they were or why they came. A niggling fear ate at her. What if they were there to see her? She wasn't even dressed yet.

Taylor jumped up and hurriedly filled the wash bowl with water. After pushing the red locks away from her face, she surveyed bloodshot eyes. She wet a washcloth and held it against them for a moment, hoping the coolness would fade the redness.

Someone rapped on her door. "Mariah, are you awake?" Frank called out.

"I'm up, but I'm not dressed." She hurried to grab her wrapper in case he came in.

"Well, get dressed. You have guests."

"Oh *shit*, they *are* here to see me!" she mumbled.

"Did you say something?"

"I'll be right down. You can come in if you'd like." She quickly pulled her robe closed and raked fingers through her tangled hair. She wanted to plunge her head into the bowl of water and drown herself. She didn't even the correct answers to Frank's questions and now she had a new bunch of strangers waiting to grill her.

He entered with huge smile on his face, seeming way too cheerful for so early in the morning. "It's the Ladies' Angelical Society. They've come to pay a visit to see if they can help out while you recover."

"Ladies what kind of society? I don't even know what that means. And recover? I am recovered... well almost." She plopped down on the bed and crossed her arms.

"Mariah, don't getting' your nose out of joint, and stop actin' like a child. They're your friends. You need to get dressed and come downstairs to the parlor."

The parlor? Thank goodness I dusted in there.

What did one say to strange women who apparently thought they knew her? She felt like a child being forced to take a bite of a dreaded vegetable. She felt Frank's impatience.

"Oh, all right!" she snapped. "Tell them I'll be right down."

Frank winked and left the room. She crossed to the armoire and selected a flowered print dress, pulled it on, then smoothed the skirt. Her gaze rested on the ridiculous selection of shoes in the closet. She certainly didn't want to suffer the pain and agony of the high button ones. And she thought high-heels were torture.

She slipped her feet into the only pair of low tops there. "No one can see my feet anyhow," she mumbled.

Even those were stiff and uncomfortable. Mariah certainly had no fashion sense or eye for comfort. In fact, her whole closet was a fashion disaster. Taylor snapped her fingers. "See, another clue I'm not Frank's wife. I hate her clothes *and* her shoes.

She stood before the mirror, yanked a brush through her disheveled hair, then pulled it back and tied it with a ribbon that complimented her dress. She paused for a moment and stared at her image. Why couldn't she believe it was her face she saw? It wasn't an ugly one, but one makeup could work wonders on.

She pinched her cheeks until they turned red,

copying what she'd once seen in a western movie. The rosy color faded almost immediately, and with a sigh, she turned from the mirror and peered down at her dowdy attire. "Well, this is as good as it gets."

Pausing for a moment, she grasped the railing at the top of the stairs. *God, help me say the right thing. The last thing I need is anyone else thinking I've lost my mind.* She descended, feeling as though she'd been sentenced to the gallows instead of having tea with Mariah's friends.

She took a deep breath before walking into the parlor, and the moment she appeared, the women converged on her, asking a million questions. As each one hugged her, she tried not to stiffen. She reminded herself to act like she knew them, but wondered how when she didn't even know their names.

Frank entered and put his arm around her shoulders. "Ladies, ladies," he spoke over the chatter. "Give my wife a little breathin' space. She's had a bad bump on her head and you'll have to excuse her if she doesn't remember everything. The doc says it'll take some time, but her memory'll come back."

Taylor released a pent up breath and smiled. God bless Frank for being home and not out on the range. He looked at her and winked. "How about if I go put on a kettle of water so you ladies can have some tea?"

* * * *

Taylor bid the women goodbye and thanked them for coming. Clare, Francis, Maggie, LewAnn, Sarah, Opal, Minnette and Sassy each waited her turn for Frank's help to get back into the wagons. Taylor felt a little annoyed at the way some of them brazenly flirted with him, but then reminded herself he wasn't her husband. Why did she care?

Once they were all aboard, they called out their good-byes and headed their wagons toward the gate. Taylor stood on the porch and waved until she lost sight of them in swirling dust. Exhausted, she plopped down in her wicker chair. "Oh my lord. That was tiring."

Frank laughed and took a seat next to her. "Yep, I can imagine. All that hen cluckin' wore me out just listening."

She smiled. "Thanks for coming to my rescue. I don't think I could have managed an explanation."

"Glad I could help."

"Well, your help is still needed."

"For what?"

"Sassy forced me to promise we'd come to town for the next church social."

Frank eyes sparkled. "Really? That'll be great. When?"

"Next Sunday." Dread sat like a stone in the pit of her stomach. The last time she'd gone to church was when she married David. She imagined people in hell putting on coats for the upcoming freeze.

CHAPTER TWENTY-TWO

Denver, Colorado—2003

Mariah was almost asleep when the bedroom door opened. Frozen with fear, she lay perfectly still and listened to footsteps coming closer. She considered screaming. Instead, she waited, with breath halted, afraid to roll over and look.

The side of the bed sagged with the weight of another's body. The fragrance of David's after-shave wafted past her nose. She relaxed, knowing it was only him and not one of the intruders she'd heard about on the evening news. The world had turned into a much uglier place than she recalled.

He touched her shoulder. "Taylor, are you asleep?"

His warm breath caressed the side of her face. "Yes…no! What do you want?"

"I can't take it any longer. Sleeping in the guest room is killing me. I belong in here with you." He stretched out next to her.

Moonlight filtered through the blinds, providing a dim glow to the room's interior and casting striations upon his face. She sat, but inched backwards. "You promised you wouldn't rush me."

"I know I did, but I can't take it any more. It's been over a month since we last made love. It's never been this long before. Hell, you were always the one all over me. I never knew how much I'd miss that."

His description was unthinkable. "I would never make the first move. It isn't ladylike. My mother taught me better than that."

He reached for her hand. "Taylor, even your mother jokes about you about being so sexual. Just relax and let it happen. Maybe it will help you remember how much we love each other."

He attempted to pull her closer.

Mariah stiffened and put her hands against his chest. "My mother would never joke about something so personal. I can't make love to you, and I won't. Please, David, just stop."

He sighed. "Taylor, I love you."

Mariah held him at arm's length. "You just don't understand, David. I am *not* Taylor! Why can't you understand that? I've never been with anyone except my husband, Frank. Making love with you would be a betrayal, not to mention a sin."

"But what about me? Don't I matter? You tell me you aren't Taylor, but every time I look at you, that's who I see."

"I can't help that. I'm sorry. Honestly."

He grabbed her hand and pressed it against his groin. "Feel that? You make this happen. My body wants you. Let me love you, Taylor. Don't push me away, I'm begging you."

Mariah jerked her hand away from his hardness and scrambled from the bed. Her body shook with anger as she glared at him. "I want you to stop, David! I mean it. For the last time, I am *not* your wife."

A dejected look, visible even in the dim light, crept over his face. He sat up. "Okay, okay. I know I promised not to push myself on you and I'll keep that vow. Really, I will. You can trust me."

Mariah took a breath and plopped back onto the bed's edge. "I know this is difficult for you. It is for both of us. If I let you stay here, can we just talk about Frank and Taylor? Then you'll see just how real Frank is... and I'd like to get to know Taylor better. Can we just talk?"

A half-crooked smile formed on David's lips. "Well, it's better than being all alone across the hall."

The both stretched out, but left ample space between their bodies.

Mariah inched beneath the covers, pulling them up beneath her chin like a protective barrier. She turned to her side and rested her head on the pillow. "Tell me what you miss most about Taylor... other than intimacy."

Still atop the blankets, he folded his hands behind his head and crossed his ankles. "Hmm! That's a hard question. My life with Taylor is intimacy. Like I said, she's a pretty aggressive woman and not just in the bedroom. I think I miss her sassiness the most."

"I've never been a sassy woman, although I do know one with that name. Sassy Clinton, she's part of my church group." Mariah chuckled.

"I'm not sure I believe in your fantasy world, but I'll play along. Frank must be quite a man to hold your heart so dearly. What do you miss about him?"

"Oh, he is quite a man. As honest as the day is long, strong, yet gentle, and he makes me laugh. He's great with the children. I think what I miss the most are the evenings we spend on the front porch after the children are in bed."

David cocked his head to the side. "Taylor and I plan on having children someday. I'd like it to be soon, but she's got other plans right now."

Detecting his sadness, Mariah reached out and

touched his arm. "I'm sure you'll have lots of children, and you'll probably be a wonderful father."

He studied her face for the longest time then shook his head. "I can't believe we're having this conversation. You almost make me believe that Frank really exists.

* * * *

Sunlight flooded through a gap in the vertical blinds on the sliding door. Mariah turned away from the glare and glanced to the other side of the bed where David still slept. They had stayed awake, talking until almost dawn. After everything he'd shared with her, she was beginning to know Taylor quite well. She wished David believed in Frank as much as she did Taylor.

True to his word, David remained a perfect gentleman and had even asked permission to climb under the covers. His soft snore sounded in the silence. She gazed upon his sleeping form, appreciating his good looks and understanding how a woman could be attracted to him. Did Taylor love him as much as he loved her?

The constant rise and fall of his chest coincided with little snorts that flared his nostrils. He stirred unwelcome feelings that Mariah knew were a result of missing Frank. Still, she had an urge to reach over and touch his cheek, to brush aside the one lock of hair resting on his forehead. She reminded herself David was a good friend and nothing more, and she didn't want to make him believe otherwise.

Being careful not to wake him, she edged off the bed, went into the bathroom and quietly closed the door. Her body ached from lack of a full night's rest. A shower seemed like a good idea. While waiting for the water to warm, she searched for her toothbrush. She stood before the mirror and pondered the face staring back at her, and again wondered about Taylor's feelings for David. "Wherever you are, Taylor," Mariah whispered, "I hope you know how much David misses you. You're a very lucky woman." Strange, but talking aloud to Taylor seemed almost normal.

Mariah opened the shower door and stepped into the steaming mist. The hot water soothed her body and relaxed her taut muscles. By the time she finished shampooing, the water had turned cold. She dried off, wrapped herself in the towel and tiptoed back into the bedroom. While opening the drawer to get clean underclothes, David stirred.

He stretched his hands above his head and opened his mouth in a half yawn, half sigh. Acting as though seeing her in a towel was normal, he smiled. "Good morning, sunshine. You're up bright and early."

She modestly clutched her wrap tighter and sidled toward the closet. "Guess I had enough sleep." Why hadn't she taken her clothes into the bathroom with her?

David sat and ran his hands through his thick hair. "You look fresh and clean. A shower might be just what I need, too. Tell you what, afterwards I'll take you out for breakfast."

He jumped up in a display of energy she wished she felt, grabbed his robe from its hook on the closet door and strode into the bathroom.

"Yikes! This water's cold," he soon yelled.

She'd forgotten to warn him.

"Sorry. I didn't mean to use it all," she called as she smoothed the rumpled bed. Recalling David's behavior last night, she snickered. Maybe a cold shower would do him good.

* * * *

In an attempt to kill time while David dressed, Mariah meandered through the house. She focused again on all the wondrous gadgets and contraptions surrounding her, and paused for a moment gaze out the kitchen window. The colorful flowers blooming in the back yard reminded her of the prairie and home. Thoughts of her family filled her mind. What they were doing right now? If loneliness could break a heart, surely hers was shattering.

Her reflection stared back at her. Tears rimmed her eyes and distorted her vision. Suddenly, an image of Frank's face hazily appeared next to hers in the window. He looked so real she reached to touch his cheek, but her hand stroked cold glass instead.

"Wow, I feel better," David said from behind. "I'm hungry, how about you? What do you feel like having?"

She choked back her emotions and knuckled the wetness from her eyes before he noticed. "There are so many choices," she said, turning. "Can I wait and choose when we get there?"

* * * *

David walked around to Taylor's side of the car, opened the door and helped her out. She paused and gazed at the sign atop the building—*IHOP*.

"What does that mean?" she asked.

He sighed. Tired of questions to which she should already know the answers, he feigned patience. "You remember, *IHOP*. It's your favorite pancake house."

"*No!* I don't." Tightness ridged her jaw.

He held open the restaurant door and followed her

inside. At times, this woman he thought to be his wife, seemed like a stranger. As usual, she appeared to be in awe of even the simplest things. Even an unimpressive coffee shop.

When they reached their table, she paused and scanned the room, appearing to look for a familiar face, but that made no sense. David cleared his throat. "Your chair, my love."

She sat and pulled a napkin into her lap, and without a word, studied the menu.

David peered over the top of his. "I'm surprised you even bothered opening the menu. Usually you just order strawberry pancakes."

She shook her head. "I would *never* do that. Strawberries make me break out in a rash. Last time I tried one, I turned almost as red as the berry and itched for days."

His shoulders sagged. She had an explanation for everything. There was no winning with her. He reached across the table and touched her hand. "Taylor, I'm at my wit's end here. I've taken a leave of absence to help you get better, but it seems we aren't getting anywhere. What's happening to us?"

Rather than pull her hand away as she normally did, she held on. "David, I've said I'm sorry a hundred times, but I don't know why I continue to apologize. Believe me; this is all as strange to me as it is to you. Think about it. How could we have conjured up the people we talked about last night? Surely you can see that even though I may look like your wife, I have nothing in common with her. I'm Mariah Cassidy. Wherever your Taylor is, I'm sure she misses you terribly. I'm so frustrated I want to scream."

He hung his head. She was right again. No matter how much he wanted to believe she was Taylor, she wasn't. All the differences he'd noticed between her and his wife haunted him.

Whether it was the accident or divine intervention, the woman across from him was not his Taylor. His gazed locked with hers. "I think it's time for us to take Dr. Shaw's advice and contact the psychotherapist he recommended. If that's okay with you, *Ms. Cassidy*, I'll call and make the appointment."

Mariah's heart fluttered. He finally believed her. She was about to respond when the waitress came to the table. "You folks ready to order?"

CHAPTER TWENTY-THREE

Colorado Territory—1872

Frank whistled as he hitched old Gert to the buggy—until scenes of his last trip to town flashed through his mind. He stopped and questioned the wisdom of making this trip, but pacified himself, thinking it would be highly unlikely to have another mishap. He brushed aside his apprehensive feelings and grabbed the harness on the old mare and led her out of the barn. Maybe today would be the day she remembered him and their life together.

* * * *

Taylor primped in front of the mirror. Today, especially, she wanted to look her best. Recalling last week's visitors, she wanted assure she was the best-looking woman at the social. She pushed a stray lock of red hair from her face and grimaced. Red hair would never be her favorite, but she had no choice. Despite the color, she found the natural curl a nice touch. She was used to paying money for them in the past. At least, she still believed it was her past. She had no proof of anything she believed to be true. She had no choice but to try to enjoy today.

After making sure every hair was in place, she paused for a moment then laughed aloud. "Why are you going to all this trouble, you big dummy? Your hair is doomed anyhow.

You're you're going by buggy, not in a Lexus."

To make sure that her bow was perfect and all her buttons fastened, she made one last twirl in front of the mirror. Satisfied, she made her way downstairs and out the door.

Frank's eye widened when he saw her. He whistled. "Are you ready to go, pretty lady?"

Taylor curtsied. "Thank you, sir. I believe I am. Maybe on the way there you can tell me what to expect. I'm embarrassed to say I haven't ever been to a social."

His smile faded. "That's not true. You just don't remember."

He took her elbow and helped her into the buggy, "Are you ever going to remember?" he mumbled.

Once seated, she scowled at him. "I do remember. Just not the things you think I should."

"Do you have everything?" He asked, changing the subject. His smile seemed forced.

"I think so. Is there something I need, that I don't know about?"

He thought for a moment. "Well, a Bible might be fittin'. It *is* a church social."

"Hmmm, I never thought about that. Sorry. Since I don't know where you keep it, you'll have to go get it."

Frank disappeared into the house and reappeared, carrying the family Bible. He handed it to her. "Maybe this will jog your memory."

The book looked familiar. "This was on the parlor table, wasn't it? I remember moving it when I dusted in there."

"Yep. You might want to take a look at it. You've recorded all our family history in there—births, deaths, marriages."

While Frank walked around to climb in, she began

turning pages. None of the notations meant a thing. She stared at the handwriting. "Yes, there really is a history here, but this isn't my handwriting."

"It has to be. You're the one who kept the records."

"Well, since I don't have a pen or pencil handy, I can't prove it, but when we get home, remind me to write something for you. You can compare. Maybe then you'll believe me."

"Let's not argue now. I don't want anything to spoil the day, so can we call a truce? Later we'll compare the writing, but for now, let's just go and have a good time. We deserve it."

He snapped the reins and Gert responded. The buggy wheels turned with a hair-raising creak that eventually faded.

* * * *

After an hour of crossing an endless sea of prairie grass turned brown from the sun, Taylor began to fidget. "How much longer till we get there?"

She stifled a giggle, mentally comparing her question to the very one she asked as a child in the back seat of her parents' car. David's voice broke into her reverie.

"Not too much farther. We've been lucky. It's unseasonably cool for this time of the year. It looks like we may even get a storm in the next day or so. See those clouds building off to the north?"

She ducked her head and looked out from under the canopy. Far in the distance, ominous, gray thunderclouds piled atop each other. "Well, I hope it doesn't rain today."

"Don't worry, it probably won't. Usually takes a while for the clouds to move in." He pulled back on the reins and stopped atop a hill. "Well, there it is, Beaver Creek."

Taylor looked down at the small community lost in the middle of nothingness—one large main street, buildings on each side, and a scattering of homes dotting the landscape around the town. "Beaver Creek, huh? Not very big, is it?"

"Nope, but it's the closest place for us to get supplies without having to travel for hours. Lots of nice folks hereabouts."

"So, if you really wanted to go to a town—a big one—where would you go?"

"Denver City, I reckon. It's not the biggest, but it's the closest."

"Where is it from here?"

"Farther north. There was a terrible flood back in '64 that pert near took 'em off the map, but the town rallied and rebuilt. I'll bet there's well over two thousand people living round those parts now. Seems to be prospering."

Taylor's mouth gaped. Two thousand people? The city she remembered was miles and miles of buildings, homes, highways and cars. She shook her head, amazed that nothing she believed to be true was evidenced by what lay before her. A chill passed through her, and she pulled her shawl around her shoulders. She looked at Frank and forced a grin. "Well, we best not just sit here. I don't want to be late to my first church social."

Gert trudged along pulling the carriage down Main Street. Taylor glanced from side to side, hardly believing her eyes. Waking up in a ranch house was shocking enough, but now she truly felt she'd taken a giant step back in time. She expected to see John Wayne lumbering along the plank walkway, or Little Joe, Hoss and Ben riding in from the Ponderosa.

Horses tied to the hitching rails lined the street, and all the women strolling along wore dresses similar to those she'd found in Mariah's armoire. "Shit, this has to be a bad dream."

Frank jerked his head around and glared at her. "That's hardly appropriate talk for someone headed for a church social."

She covered her mouth, unaware she'd muttered her thoughts aloud. Her cursing really bothered him, but it had become habit. "I'm sorry. I'm honestly trying to clean up my mouth, but I'm having a hard time absorbing all this Old West stuff."

He shook his head. "What do you mean? This should be all familiar to you, but for the life of me, I'm trying to understand why it isn't."

He reined Gert to a halt in front of the church—the last building on the street before more flat prairie land. Although small, the tall steeple housed a fair-sized bell with a pristine white cross adorning the very top. People they'd passed on the street arrived and went inside; most carried a dish of some sort.

Frank came around and helped her down, then went to tend Gert. Taylor stepped onto the plank walkway, straightened her dress, and ran her fingers through her windblown hair. She took a breath to calm her runaway heart. Facing more strangers wasn't exactly something she welcomed. She jumped when Frank touched her elbow.

"Shall we?"

Yet another couple entered the church carrying a covered dish. They smiled and waved before disappearing through the door. "Frank," Taylor whispered, "should we have brought food to share?

"I reckon we should've."

"Well, why didn't you say something? We're going to be the only freeloaders here."

"Free whatters?"

"Oh, never mind. It's too late now." She flipped her hair over her shoulder and took another deep breath.

Frank put his hand in the middle of her back and hurried her inside. Motioning for her to sit in the pew closest to the door, he scooted in next to her. The bench was hard and uncomfortable, and more people crowded into the almost full church. With the doors closed, it didn't take long before the air turned uncomfortably warm and stale. Taylor felt claustrophobic and struggled to breathe.

Pastor Amos, as she'd learned his name, walked behind the pulpit and raised his arms. Everyone stood and, with hymnal in hand, began to sing. Taylor fumbled through pages, trying to find the right song, but didn't recognize the lyrics at all. Frank's baritone voice crooned pleasantly next to her—his voice a nice mix with those surrounding them. She finally gave up looking and mouthed the words as best she could. When the song ended, everyone sat.

Like an antsy child, Taylor fidgeted on the hard wooden seat, wishing she was anywhere else. She already dreaded the long ride home, and pictured the monotony.

"I'm so pleased to see Mariah Cassidy among us today."

Taylor snapped to attention as soon as she heard the pastor call out Mariah's name.

"Hallelujah!" he proclaimed. "Let's all welcome her and give thanks to the Lord that she's back among the flock."

All eyes turned to her; Taylor felt her face heat. She managed a crooked smile, much like that of a little girl caught stealing cookies.

Everyone applauded.

She straightened in her seat and nodded in appreciation, hoping she hadn't missed anything important that had been said. Daydreaming was always something she did when she became bored. She forced herself to pay attention for the remainder of the service.

After a short sermon and a few announcements, the Pastor invited the congregation out onto the walkway between the church and the rectory. Long tables along the wall held a bounty of food, and plates and utensils were ready at the end. On a separate table, a large punch bowl stood filled to capacity with lemonade. Fresh fruit slices floated on top. Frank pointed out a short, stocky woman to Taylor. "That's Mrs. Amos, the Pastor's wife."

The woman appeared to be less than five feet tall and almost as wide. Despite her ample size, she moved easily from person to person, welcoming each and encouraging all to fill their plates. When she noticed Taylor, Mrs. Amos made a beeline in her direction and warmly embraced her. "Mariah, my sweet. I'm so happy to see you here. We've all been praying for your recovery."

Taylor tried hard to relax and act naturally. "Thank you, Mrs. Amos. It's nice to be here. I'm so sorry I didn't bring a dish to share."

Mrs. Amos patted her shoulder. "There, there, my dear, don't you fret. I heard all about your terrible experience. We wouldn't expect you to bring something. We're just glad to have you here with us. Please eat and enjoy."

Taylor and Frank filled their plates and took a seat on the rock wall next to the rectory. While munching on the tasty array of food, she watched the children play. Running and giggling, they dodged in and out between the visiting adults, surprisingly unnoticed. Their giggles were contagious and she smiled. Frank intently watched one young boy about the same age as Jacob. Taylor nudged him with her elbow. "I know you must really miss the children. Why don't you make a trip tomorrow and bring them home? I'm sure they miss you, too."

He swallowed a bite of food and flashed a broad smile. "Thanks, I think I will. It isn't the same without them around. Are you sure you'll be able to handle the questions they have? You know they don't understand this any more than we do."

She chuckled. "I'm fine with it. I guess you haven't noticed—I'm starting to mellow a bit."

CHAPTER TWENTY-FOUR

Denver, Colorado—2003

David and Mariah walked down the long carpeted hallway leading to Dr. Ramone's office. Brightly painted pictures hung on both sides of the walls, bringing out matching colors in the plush floor covering. The trip there had been stressful. During the ride, Mariah struggled with how to explain this strange turn of events to the analyst without appearing to be totally crazed.

"Suite 203. Here we are." David reached for the doorknob.

Mariah took a deep breath and entered. A young woman slid open a glass partition. "Hello. May I help you?"

David approached the counter. "Yes, I'm David Morgan." Gesturing behind him, he said, "And this … this is Mariah Cassidy. We have an appointment with Dr. Ramone."

Hearing her own name was music to Mariah's ears. Twice now, David had actually used it. She smiled at the woman.

"We've been expecting you. Please, will you and Ms. Cassidy have a seat and I'll let the doctor know you're here."

Mariah's knees wobbled. She had no idea how to begin her story for the doctor, and gladly took a seat. David sat next to her. He leaned on his knees and rubbed his palms together, appearing as anxious as she felt.

The scratching noise he made seemed increasingly

loud in the silence. She reached over and grabbed one of his hands. "David, please relax. You're making me nervous."

He swiped his palms on his pant legs and leaned back. "Sorry, I just don't know what to expect."

"That's a surprise."

David's head snapped around. "Just exactly what does that mean?"

"I'm the one locked in this time zone. I'm just saying, you seem to have a better grasp on things than I do."

The tenseness seemed to drain from his shoulders. "Let's not argue about things right now. This hasn't been easy for either of us. I do concede, it's probably been harder on you, but it hasn't been a picnic for me either. Let's both take a deep breath and try to get through this."

The door next to the counter opened and the young lady appeared. "Right this way. Dr. Ramone will see you now."

Mariah felt thankful David stood first and helped her up on quivering legs. She really wanted to run in the other direction, but instead followed behind as they were led to the doctor's office.

In comparison to the cheery hallway, Dr. Ramone's office was dark and sedate. A petite woman, looking to be about forty, sat behind a large desk that dwarfed her when she stood. One side of the mahogany surface held neatly stacked folders and the displayed various framed photographs. One of a young girl with hair the color of Callie's brought a lump to Mariah's throat. She swallowed hard.

"Good morning, I'm Doctor Ramone." The petite woman smiled. "You must be Mr. Morgan and Ms. Cassidy."

David nodded. "Yes. It's very nice to meet you." He offered his hand.

Dr. Ramone locked palms with him then motioned

toward two large chairs in front of her desk. "Please, have a seat."

Mariah's knees threatened to buckle. She smiled at the doctor and dropped into the leather chair next to David. "Thank you." Her voice came out in a whisper.

The doctor sat behind her desk and picked up a pen and pad. "Tell me what brings you in today. My notes show that my friend, Dr. Shaw, referred you."

"Yes, he treated my... treated Ms. Cassidy after a bad car accident." David answered.

He paused for a moment. "Let me see if I can word this so it makes sense."

Mariah flashed a pleading look at him. It was a sure thing she didn't want to try to explain the madness.

While David pondered his choice of words, Dr. Ramone turned to Mariah. "Ms. Cassidy you were injured in an automobile accident? How badly?"

"D-Dr. Ramone, I-I don't know how else to present the whole story other than starting from the very beginning." The words sputtered from David's mouth and his brow furrowed. "So please bear with me. If it doesn't make sense to you, then you'll know exactly how we've felt for the past month."

* * * *

The doctor's eyes widened, but she furiously made notes. When David finished the story, she looked to Mariah and got a validating nod.

The doctor put her pen aside and leaned back in her chair. "So, let me see if I understand this correctly. Your wife is Taylor Morgan, and she looks just like the person sitting next to you, but the person sitting next to you is not your wife. She is really Mariah Cassidy?"

"That's right." David sat forward in his chair.

The doctor massaged the bridge of her nose. "You say that Taylor suffered a serious head injury in an auto mishap and when she regained consciousness in the hospital, she claimed to be Mariah Cassidy, not your wife, Taylor?"

"Yes."

"And, Mariah." The doctor looked at her. "You say you are married to Frank Cassidy, live on a ranch, have two children and..." The doctor paused and took a breath while scanning her notes. "Hmmm, and the year you last remember is 1872. Is that right?"

Mariah wrung her hands. "Yes, that's exactly what I remember. No one wants to believe I've never seen cars, or big buildings like these, or dishwashers, or a television, or..."

Dr. Ramone stood and paced behind her chair. "Okay, Ms. Cassidy. I believe you, but I'm not sure why I do. What I would like to do to confirm the story is to put you under hypnosis."

Mariah stiffened in her chair. "What exactly is that?"

"Don't worry, it's painless. It's a state of relaxation that allows me to question your inner mind. When it's over, you'll probably remember everything we talked about. Are you okay with that?"

Mariah glanced over at David, seeking guidance.

His eyes softened and he gave an encouraging nod. "In order to make any sense of this we have to do whatever Dr. Ramone thinks is best. I'll be right here with you."

Mariah looked back at the doctor and shrugged. "Okay." Using the word felt strange, but she'd heard it so often it had become part of her speech. "I don't think I have any other choice at this point."

CHAPTER TWENTY-FIVE

Colorado Territory—1872

Taylor found the social thoroughly enjoyable. She especially relished the time spent with other women. She compared their relaxed lives to hers as a hustling attorney— that life that seemed a million miles away. Before now, she believed the most important achievements were prestige and money, but living in Mariah Cassidy's shoes made those things seem a lot less important. She chuckled. She literally lived in Mariah's shoes, ugly though they were.

It was after three o'clock when Frank invaded the group of giggling women. "It's going to take us a while to get home. We'd better get moving if we want to get there before dark."

Taylor reluctantly bid farewell to her newfound friends, exchanged hugs and invitations for future visits. She was starting to accept this might be her life from now on. It really wouldn't be such a bad one if only David was part of it. Frank helped her into the buggy and she adjusted her skirt around her.

He shook hands with the Pastor and tipped his hat to Mrs. Amos. "Thanks so much for hosting the social. Mariah and I had a great time."

Mrs. Amos reached up and patted his hand. "You're welcome, Frank. I'm just so happy to see that beautiful bride of yours up and around. You know, we miss seeing you and the family in church occasionally."

His face reddened. "I know we should come more often, but the trip is such a far piece. We do try to make it once a month. I'm pretty sure God understands. Don't you?"

"I'm pretty sure he's pleased whenever you visit," the Pastor added, backing away from the rig.

As the Gert trotted away from the church, the Amos' stood on the walkway and waved goodbye. Taylor waved back through the canopy opening until the couple was no longer in sight. She turned, smoothed her skirt and folded her hands in her lap. "That was really fun. I had a nice time. Thanks for bringing me. Did you enjoy yourself?"

"Yep." He rippled the reins. "Like I said, there are lots of nice folks hereabouts."

From beneath the canopy, Taylor eyed the threatening pillars in the sky. She pulled her shawl more snugly around her shoulders. "Those clouds look mighty angry. I thought you said it would take a while for them to move in." She glanced over to check his reaction.

"Normally, it does, but these appear to be coming a might faster than normal." He pushed his hat back and eyed the sky more closely. "I'd say we might get a little wet before we get home."

"Shit! I-I mean shoot. I hate being wet and cold, and all I have is this thin shawl." She screwed her lips frown.

"Nice to see you're correctin' your language. I really appreciate it since I'm planning on fetchin' the children home. And don't pout, there's a blanket and a poncho under the seat, just in case."

Taylor smiled. "I wasn't pouting. I was just... Okay, so maybe I was. But I do hate being wet and cold."

"Among so many other things," he muttered, giving

the reins a more urgent snap.

* * * *

The wind swirled tiny pieces of dry prairie grass along the ground and hurled them into the buggy. To keep his hat from being blown away, Frank pushed it down over his eyes. From beneath the lowered brim he noticed Taylor pull her shawl over the top of her bonnet.

His hands firmly on the reins kept Gert trotting along at an even speed—she was much too old to run. The north wind made an eerie sound as it passed through the opening in the back of the canopy. Taylor mumbled to herself, "Dumb idea... hole…put window…very bright…"

Frank heard only bits and pieces. "What'd you say?"

"Nothing. Doesn't matter. I was complaining again. Did I mention I also hate wind?"

He chuckled, but kept a wary eye on the sky. He wondered where they might seek shelter if it became necessary. There wasn't much between them and home.

The force of the wind grew stronger, swaying the buggy from side to side. Gert struggled against the headwind. Frank reached under the seat and grabbed the poncho. "Here, you'd better put this on. It looks like I misjudged the storm's arrival."

Taylor pulled the heavy woven material over her head. "This isn't exactly the fashion statement I wanted to make."

"Well, it's only you, me and Gert, so I wouldn't worry about it. You might wanna fetch the blanket and wrap it round your legs."

He'd barely finished his sentence before the rain started. Blowing in front the front, it drenched Taylor's face and soaked the blanket, but at least the poncho afforded some protection. Ahead, Frank spied an outcropping of rocks just high enough to provide some respite from the torrential rain, or so he thought. Despite the canopy, the wind continued to blow rain in from front and side. Water drizzled from the brim of his hat. "Well, this wasn't a great idea. I hoped to keep you from gettin' wetter, but I see there's no reason to sit here. We may as well keep movin'. At least we'll be getting closer to home."

Holding his hat with one hand to secure it from a sudden gust of wind, he snapped the reins with the other. "Giddyap, Gert."

* * * *

Frank reined Gert to a halt next to the porch. "Go ahead and get out. I'll be in after I dry this old mare off a bit."

Taylor threw off the soaked blanket and, wrestling with her drenched skirt, tried to alight. It was as though her legs had developed a second skin. The poncho had provided little protection from the driving rain. Water cascaded from her soaked bonnet and sent little rivers of water snaking down her face. She stood in a puddle on the porch and laughed. "I appreciate the courtesy, but I don't think walking from the barn would have made much difference."

"Well, give me credit for *trying* to be a gentleman. I'm sorry the ride home was so awful."

Leaving a trail of water in her wake, she stepped inside the house, stopping on the braided rug inside the door. She hugged herself.

Oh thank goodness. To be warm again.

She stripped herself of her wet garments where she

stood then carefully carried them across the kitchen floor, and put them in the laundry tub. Grabbing a towel, she bent over and let her wet tresses hang free while trying to remove the excess moisture. "The only thing worse then red hair is wet, red hair," she mumbled.

"Ahem," Frank announced from the back door. "You do know I'm in the house? I have to admit I like the view."

His voice startled her. The chemise she wore left very little to the imagination and her position obviously displayed far too much. She quickly straightened and wrapped herself in the towel. Her cheeks heated.

"Well, I do now. Please take your wet stuff off before you cross the floor. Remember, I just mopped." Listening to herself speak, she wondered when her personality changed to fit her new face.

He stepped out of his boots, stripped off his blue jeans and shirt and stood in his long johns. "What do I do with my wet clothes, ma'am?" he asked.

"Put them here in the wash tub—and be careful where you drip." She tried not to laugh at him.

He tiptoed across the floor. "My, my, haven't we changed. I can imagine what you would have told me to do with them a couple of weeks ago."

"I told you I'm mellowing. I figure I can't explain what's happened and I can't control where I am, but I can try to keep my sanity. There could be worse places to be."

"Well, thanks a lot."

"You know what I meant. I'm very thankful you've been so supportive. I know this has been just as hard on you. Every morning, when I wake, I wish I could explain all this away. I've run everything through my mind a million times and still come up with *nada*, nothing, zip!"

"I suppose all three of those words mean the same thing?"

"Oh dear, you're starting to figure me out." She chuckled. "You do have to agree since I've been here, you have learned some new words."

"That's for sure, but some I prefer not to use."

"Listen, I've toned it down a lot." She reached for a kitchen towel and wrapped it around the ends of her drippy hair. "You have no idea how bad it could have been."

They both laughed. Taylor gazed into Frank's eyes and realized they'd just shared something. "Look at us. We're laughing like nothing is wrong."

"I know, it actually felt good, didn't it?"

She nodded. "But that doesn't change things, does it? We can enjoy each other as long as we understand we're married to other people. I know it must be hard for you because I look like your wife, but as handsome as you are, you aren't my David—and I miss him."

"Believe me, I do understand. You may look like my Mariah, but I'm finally seeing you're really nothin' like her."

"Really? And how are we different?" She was pretty sure she already knew.

"Mariah is a prim and proper lady. I've never heard her say a cuss word. Even when she's mad at me, she won't argue. You're a tad bit too spirited and mouthy."

Taylor put her hands on her hips. "Mouthy? You haven't even seen the real me."

"From where I'm standing, I see quite a bit of you."

She glanced down and realized her towel had fallen to the floor. "Gee, I guess I have become way too comfortable with you."

He chuckled. "It appears that way. Why don't we

change into something comfortable, have a bite to eat and talk a little more? This is nice."

"Okay, deal. Last one up the stairs has to cook." Before she finished the challenge, she darted for the staircase, leaving Frank standing in the kitchen.

"Hey," he called after her. "I said we could have a bite to eat. I didn't say I would cook."

Taylor reached the landing, laughing and out of breath. He had no idea how lucky he was to lose the contest.

CHAPTER TWENTY-SIX

Denver, Colorado—2002

Dr. Ramone pulled the draperies closed, making her office even darker. She showed Mariah to the chaise along the wall. "Please lie down and get comfortable."

Doing as instructed, she reclined but fidgeted, trying to find the right position. She gazed up and grimaced at the ugly painting hanging above her and wondered why someone would frame a bunch of circles and splashes. With eyes closed, she willed her heartbeat to slow.

At the sound of the doctor pulling her chair closer, Maria stiffened. She expelled a silent breath. What had she agreed to?

"Now, my dear, I want you to listen very closely." The woman's tone helped Mariah relax. "Are you comfortable?"

Mariah opened her eyes and nodded. "Yes."

"Listen to my voice and do as I say. I want you to focus on deep and even breathing, feel each inhalation flowing through your entire body. Starting with your toes. Pictures them in your mind, then sense the muscles under the skin relaxing, and let your toes feel free. Now moving up to your ankles. Notice any stress in that part of your body, and as you listen to my voice, feel that tension go away."

"Now, we're traveling up your thighs, into your hips. Let any tightness fade away as you relax your muscles. Everything is limp. Feel that sensation moving up, up, up your body. When I count to three, I want you to close your eyes and be totally relaxed. You will answer my questions freely, without fear. You're safe and nothing can harm you. One… two… three."

Mariah wasn't sure she wanted to proceed. She struggled to keep her eyes open, but they obediently closed. The doctor's voice commanded and Mariah's body obeyed. She couldn't move her arms, and her legs felt leaden.

"Mariah, do you hear me?" Dr. Ramone asked.

"Yes." Her voice was a mere whisper.

"We're going to travel backwards. Time is reversing before your eyes—rolling back. Still relaxed and safe, I want you to look closely as the years pass and tell me what you see."

"Frank. Oh, Frank darling."

"You see someone named Frank? Who is he?"

"He's my husband."

"What's he doing?"

"He's helping me into the wagon. We're going to town."

"Are you alone?"

"No, our children, Callie and Jacob, are in the back."

"What year is it now, Mariah?"

"It's 1872 of course."

"Where do you live?"

"In Colorado."

"Are you in the wagon?"

"Yes, and we're leaving the yard. We're leaving the Rocking C."

"The Rocking C? Is that what you call your home?"

"Yes. The C stands for Cassidy."

"Okay, Mariah, you're in the wagon and you're going

to town. Tell me what's happening?"

"Jacob has to go to the bathroom." Fear gripped at Mariah. "Oh my goodness, he frightened some snakes... The horses…the horses won't quiet down. Frank, make them quiet down. It's scaring me."

"Relax, Mariah, you're safe. Relax and tell me what you see," Dr. Ramone spoke in a soothing voice.

Mariah took a deep breath but her heart pounded like the hoof beats in her mind. "The horses…they're running... running fast. Frank can't stop them. Yes, yes, Frank, I'm holding on. Hold on, children. Oh dear God, we've hit something. Help me..."

Dr. Ramone touched Mariah's arm, "Deep breath, Mariah, relax. We're going to stop now. When I count to three, you'll open your eyes and remember everything we've talked about, but you're going to feel fine. One… two… three."

Mariah blinked a few times.

Dr. Ramone put her pad and pen aside, got up and opened the draperies. Muted light filtered in through the sheers. She turned to Mariah. "Do you remember what we talked about?"

Mariah sat, put her feet on the floor and fluffed the back of her hair. "Yes, my heart is still pounding like a hammer on an anvil."

Dr. Ramone looked at David, sitting quietly in the corner. "Mr. Morgan, what do you think about what you heard?"

He ran his fingers through his hair, his eyes wider than usual. "Her recounting sounded so real, even my heart is pounding. There's no way she could imagine all this, is there, Doctor?"

"Not in my opinion. Hypnosis is usually very hard to

fake, and people in a total state of relaxation tend to be very truthful—even if they don't want to be."

David stood and walked to the window. Pushing the sheer curtain aside he peered out for a moment then turned to face Dr. Ramone. "What do you make of it? What's your opinion?"

The therapist sat back down. "I'm not sure I have one yet. This is even a little startling for me. In Mariah's mind it really is 1872. I think I need to digest this a little more. What say we stop for today and make another appointment to take Mariah back where we left off?"

* * * *

David pulled the car into the garage and hit the button to close the door. As usual, he came around to let Mariah out. "Well, here we are. How are you feeling?"

She planted both feet firmly on the cement and stood. Her knees still felt weak. "No more confused than I was, but no less either."

He opened the back door and followed her inside. "Do you think Dr. Ramone helped at all?"

"Do you?"

David went to the refrigerator and pulled out a bottle of beer. "I could use one of these. Would you like one?"

"No thanks. I tried one. Don't much like the taste. I think I'll stick with Pepsi." She reached around him and grabbed a can. "So, do you?"

"Do I what?"

"Think Dr. Ramone helped the situation?"

"I'm not sure. It was certainly… stimulating to watch you undergo hypnosis. I've never seen it done before. How did it feel?" David popped open the beer bottle and jumped up to sit on the counter.

Mariah filled a glass with ice and emptied her soda into it. After a drink, she wiped her lips with the back of her hand. "It was strange. I heard her talking to me, saw everything so clearly in my mind, yet I could only do what she asked of me."

"Do you have a problem going back again?" he asked. "Remember, we have a second appointment day after tomorrow."

"I don't mind going back, but I'm not sure what good it's going to do. I woke up in a strange place and I've been here ever since. I have memories of a husband who looks nothing like you, but you tell me I look exactly like your wife. If you say I'm confused, I have to agree."

"I think both of feel that way. I know seeing Doctor Ramone is difficult for you, but we have to find out if things are going to stay this way. I need to go back to work. It takes money to live. As much as I would like to stay home every day, I can't. The company has been kind enough to let me take family leave, and luckily we have money in the bank to cover our expenses. But it won't last forever."

Mariah shook her head. "You know, I don't even know where you work or what you do. How strange. We've shared a home and our lives for over a month—even shared a bed—but there's still so much I don't know about you."

David jumped off the counter. "Well, maybe it's time we have a long talk and take care of that. If things don't change, we may have a quite a while to get to know one another better, but we can still start now. Let's go in the living room where it's more comfortable."

He kicked off his shoes and leaned back in his recliner. Mariah sat caddy corner to him and nestled in the comfort of the pillow-back sofa, her feet tucked under her. She pondered

David's statement about how long they might have to get to know each other. "About what you said in the kitchen... You know, we might be together a long time. How do you feel about that?"

David moved his chair back into a semi-reclining position. "I'm not sure. The only thing that has been different is the inner you. When I look at you, I see my beautiful Taylor. You are her in almost every way... better in some. So, the hard part for me is knowing you really aren't my wife and trying to make myself understand how that could be."

"You say I'm like her in almost every way? What ways am I not?"

"You have a softer side. Taylor is a spirited, ambitious, working woman. She isn't a homemaker. Doesn't like to cook or clean—she will, but she grumbles. Like I told you, she isn't a very good cook at all. You really outshine her there."

Mariah felt herself heat at his compliment and lowered her eyes. "Thank you. Frank loves my cooking, too. But there's got to be something that drew you to her. Go on, tell me more about Taylor."

He locked his hands behind his head and stared up at the ceiling. "She works mostly with men every day. Taylor's an attorney and earns a good living. She's had to learn to be aggressive to survive in the business world, and being an only child, she already had a temperamental streak."

Mariah was about to ask him to explain being an attorney when a ringing doorbell interrupted.

David disappeared in the foyer. When he came back, he carried a large bouquet of spring flowers in a crystal vase. "These are for you."

"Mariah's eyes widened. "For me?"

He sat them on the coffee table, picked the card from

among the leaves and held it out to her. "Do you want to open it?"

She took the envelope and slid the card from inside. "It says, 'Get well soon. We miss you. Your pals at the office.' What pals at the office?" She flashed him a puzzled look.

David plopped back down in his chair. "Well, I'll be darned. I never would have guessed they'd be this sensitive. After all the things Taylor's told me about them, I assumed they'd been too busy to notice she was gone. Oh, *what pals?* The guys who work with Taylor at the law firm. I believe she refers to them as jerks."

Mariah leaned forward and inhaled the fragrant aroma. "They're lovely. I've never seen such a big bunch of flowers. How in the world did they find such beautiful ones?"

"I guess you wouldn't know about florists. They're people who sell flowers for special occasions—like this…get well wishes, also weddings and funerals. They probably rake in a lot from husbands who need to make up with their wives. People pay, they deliver."

"Oh, my goodness. Who would ever think of such a thing? Flowers should be free to whoever wants them. When I wanted some, I just went out for a walk and picked them where they grew."

"Well, things have changed. People find all kinds of ways to make money these days. Most people don't have time to grow flowers, let alone pick them."

"I guess it takes more money today. I'm embarrassed to admit that I don't know much about the cost of things. Is that why you and Taylor both work?" She leaned back. "You have a very exciting life."

"Exciting? There's nothing exciting about both people working full time. You barely see each other. It seems the more you earn, the more you spend. Everybody wants to outdo everyone else. If someone has a pool, then someone else gets a pool and spa. If someone gets a new car, someone else has to have a bigger, better, more expensive one. The same with homes, televisions… almost everything. We've become a very materialistic race." He sighed. "What else do you want to know?"

"I don't know. Just keep talking. I'm learning about my future."

He smiled. "Well, let's see. Taylor is pushy, mouthy and has two bad habits that drive me crazy: being late and cussing like a drunken sailor. But, I love her so much. You wanted to know what drew me to her? She makes me laugh. She keeps me sane when it seems everything else around me is crazy. And did I mention how aggressive she is in the—"

David stopped short, a sheepish look on his face.

"In?"

"I'm sorry, I didn't want to say something improper."

"You were going to say in the bedroom, weren't you?"

"How did you know?"

"Because I'm not and I know it. I'm sure you noticed when you came to my bed the other night. I'm afraid I'm just not comfortable with my sharing myself."

"Mariah, I've apologized already, but I really am sorry for being so pushy."

She stared into her lap. "I understand. We all have needs. I'm probably not as forward as most men would like their wives to be, but I was brought up in a different time and place. Acting brazenly is considered improper. My mother was very straight-laced and I had strict rules to follow until I married Frank. Then, I didn't know anything about the facts of life, so what I do know I learned from him." She raised her gaze and shrugged. "He never complains and always acts like he's still in love with me, so I guess I'm tolerable."

David peered into her eyes. "Tolerable? You're more than tolerable. You're a passionate, beautiful woman. There's nothing wrong with being different. I'm sure if you stay in this century, you'll find out more about sex than you ever wanted to know. It's everywhere—billboards, movies, television, books."

"Do you think I'm going to stay here and never see my Frank again?" Tears welled in her eyes. "Or my children? I have two precious children. What must they being doing without their mother?"

"Please, don't cry! I don't think we have much control over the situation. We sure as hell don't understand it. Maybe it's a time travel thing. I've read about the possibility, but never believed in it, but now..."

"Time travel? I've never even heard of such a thing, but if there is, I definitely believe in it. How else would you explain my being here instead of where I belong in 1872 with my family? One minute I'm there and the next minute I'm here. How else can you explain it?" She nibbled her bottom lip.

"I can't, that's the problem. I have no explanation, no remedy, no cure, and no expectations at this point. I want you to be able to return to your family, honestly. Believe it not, I want my pushy, opinionated, veraciously sexy wife back. I'm even willing to give up your great food."

Mariah smiled. "Well, that's what I call sacrifice." She sighed. "Looks like we need to see Dr. Ramone again and give it one more shot. Maybe there's some little thing I'm overlooking."

CHAPTER TWENTY-SEVEN

Colorado Territory—1872

With their plates empty, Frank and Taylor sat at opposite ends of the table and relaxed to let dinner digest. She rubbed her stomach. "You know, you really are a very good cook. Mariah is lucky."

"Thanks. She taught me most of what I know. I don't cook very often because she loves to."

Taylor giggled. "Well, that's where we really differ. I hate anything to do with the kitchen."

Frank leaned his chair back onto its two rear legs, dug into his shirt pocket for a small sliver of wood, and picked at his front teeth. "I kind of got that feeling since you tend to avoid this part of the house."

Feeling a little ashamed, Taylor immediately got up and began clearing the table. "How about a cup of coffee in the parlor where it's a little more comfortable?"

"Sounds good to me. I'll pour." Frank started toward the stove.

Taylor reached over and grabbed the pot. "Oh no, I'll pour. I want no more of your comments about my kitchen skills."

She filled his cup and followed him into the other room.

Frank stood next to the fireplace, leaned against the mantel and looked up at the picture of Mariah. He glanced at

Taylor, sitting in the side chair, then at the picture. "You know, now that I really look at you, there is something different about you and Mariah. It's something around your eyes."

"Really?"

"Yes, Mariah's eyes always had a certain sparkle. More so, when the kids were around and she was happy, but I haven't seen that sparkle in your eyes at all."

Taylor pondered his comments. "Well, waking up in another century, with a strange man who thinks he's your husband and believes you are mother to his two children, is not something that would put a sparkle in one's eyes. Wouldn't you agree?"

He sidled over and sat on the settee. "I see your point. You've had a rough time, but we need to discuss the future. What if this is how things are gonna stay? Are you prepared to deal with that?"

She shook her head.

"You mean no, you aren't prepared?"

"I mean I haven't even given it any consideration. I figured I would wake up one morning and find out this had been a dream. Not a nightmare, just a bad dream."

He leaned forward and rested his elbows on his knees. "Well, perhaps we need to discuss it. We've woken up quite a few mornins' now and nothing seems to be changin'."

She tried to tuck her feet under her dress, but finding it much more difficult in Mariah's clothing, she gave up. "You're right. It's been a month and everything is the same. I keep thinking about my life—not Mariah's. Have I lost my job with the law firm? Has David found someone else? Does he even know I'm gone? Maybe he's in a time warp and hasn't missed me yet."

"I know it's hard. I think about Mariah every day.

Where is she? If you're here, then where is she? Does she miss me as much as I miss her?"

Taylor cringed at his remark. "It didn't seem you missed her too much the other night when you came to my bed." She immediately wanted to bite her tongue for being so crude. "I'm sorry, that was unkind. I was just as guilty and willing as you."

Frank stood and paced. "It's hard to explain. Every day, I look at you, and except for the missin' sparkle I noticed tonight, you look just like Mariah. You smell and feel like her. I'm a man with needs, and in my mind, I was just makin' love to my wife."

Taylor took a deep breath. "Then what's my excuse? You don't look anything like David. Maybe I just needed to be held, and God knows David would tell you I'm a sex fiend. Was it so bad with me?"

Frank stopped pacing and jerked around, staring at her with wide eyes. "*No*, it was wonderful! Mariah is a good wife and a willin' partner, but she's shy and reserved. That's when it really hit me you were tellin' the truth. You are her opposite. I've never had a woman be so aggressive with me."

"If I were a blushing sort of person that would make me turn red, but since I'm not, I'll just say thank you. I've never been told I was good in bed."

"What about your husband? Doesn't he tell you?" Frank sat again.

"No! We have a good sex life, but I'm the more energetic of the two of us, so I'm usually the one to start everything. I don't mind. He takes care of me."

Frank tugged at the collar on his shirt. "I can't believe we're sitting in the parlor, with the Bible right on the table in front of us, talking about such… such personal things."

"Okay, now who's being a prude?"

"I'm certainly not a prude. It's just another new experience for me. You say 'sex' like it's an everyday word. I'm used to sayin' making love."

Taylor straightened her legs, stretched her hands over her head and yawned. "Well, we aren't getting very far in this conversation about the future. We tend to keep looking backwards."

He sighed. "What do you think is going to happen? Is this fate for us? Who would have guessed that a simple trip to town would cause such a change? By the way, you never told me what you remembered before you woke up here."

Taylor rubbed the back of her neck. "All I remember is leaving home to go to work. I was doing the same thing I do every morning: take the interstate a few miles, get off, get into stop-and-go traffic, get pissed—oops, sorry! The next thing I recall is the signal light turning green and that's about it. I woke up in the bed upstairs."

"You just conjured up at least twenty questions for me: interstate, traffic, signal. But if things are meant to stay this way, you'll have a lot of time to school me."

Taylor sat up straight. "How about the day you went to town? I know you said you were in a wagon and the horses got scared. Was anything out of the ordinary other than the accident?"

Frank cupped his chin. "I remember cradling your... her head in my lap, washing away the blood and begging for a response. She never said a word."

"Did—"

"Wait!" He held up a finger. "There *was* something strange. Lightning. One bolt of lightning."

"Why is that strange?"

He snapped his fingers. "Yes, that's it. It was unusual because there were no clouds in the sky. I remember thinking the air felt strange, but the sky was clear. When I called Mariah's name, a single bolt of lightning struck the dirt not too far away from where we were."

Taylor stretched. "Well, I don't have any idea how that could cause something like this, but I do know I'm tired. We've talked for hours. Would you think me rude if I went to bed?"

"No, not at all. I'm tuckered, too. This has been a full day, and it's late. You know, I've been thinkin' 'bout what you said about bringing the children home. I've decided I'm gonna wait just a little longer. I think you and I still have some talkin' to do and decisions to make."

She covered a yawn with the back of her hand before answering. "Whatever you think is best. I just thought you might really miss them."

"I do, but I can wait a bit. I'd like to have their mother back when they come home."

Taylor moved toward the stairs. "I pray that will happen, really I do. Good night, Frank. I enjoyed today. I'll see you in the morning... but not too early."

He picked up the lantern and followed her upstairs. "Go ahead and sleep as long as you want, but I have to get up early. The boys and I have to ride out to the north pasture and get started branding the new cattle."

As she opened her bedroom door, she turned and grinned at him. "Okay, Pa, Little Joe and I will be a ridin' out to help ya."

Frank shook his head then started to close his door, but peered around it. "Good night, strange lady. Sleep well."

* * * *

Taylor tossed and turned, lost in a bad dream. "David, David," she called out. In her mind she stumbled around in a heavy fog, unable to see, unable to hear and reached out for the safety of her husband's arms.

Oh, David, my love, I can't find you. Where are you? I'm here waiting. Call my name so I know where you are.

Just as she glimpsed his face and saw the joy radiating from his eyes, the dream ended. Her breath came in gasps as she sat straight up in bed. "It was so real. I saw him."

Glancing around the moonlit room, she made out the same familiar surroundings: a wash basin, an antique mirror. It was only a dream. Still stuck in 1872, in Mariah's body, she wondered why the Lord punished her.

She lay back down and pulled the quilt up under her chin.

I'm not giving up. I'm going to get home somehow. I swear I am!

* * * *

Across the hall, Frank thought he heard Taylor call out. He listened closely but all was quiet. As tired as he was, he couldn't stop his mind from racing. Did the lightning have something to do with the mysterious happenings? He clasped his hands behind his head and stared into the darkness. Sometime before morning, he drifted off to sleep.

* * * *

Taylor opened her eyes. Memories of the dream flooded back and seemed so real. She rubbed her eyes and sighed. Why couldn't she have awakened in her own bed? Rather than try to answer the same question she'd asked herself over and over, she decided to get up and do something constructive… whatever that might be.

Pushing the covers aside, she rose and walked to the mirror. She studied Mariah's face and frowned. "If you had to have red hair," she grumbled, "why didn't you at least live in a time when they had mascara for God's sake? I look pale and washed out." As she listened to herself rant, she started to laugh. "Now I've really lost it. I actually am beginning to think this is my face."

What if this becomes the face you have to live with forever?

She pushed the thought from her mind and added more water to the wash bowl. Cupping her hands, she bent over and lavished her face with water. She repeated the process and tried to wake up, then searched blindly for the towel and found it. Static crackled as the cloth passed over her skin—her hair stuck to it. Suddenly, Frank's words from last night flashed through her mind.

Lightning!

A cold chill ran up her spine. She had to find Frank. Throwing on a wrapper, she ran down the stairs. While searching the kitchen and parlor, she remembered he had gone to brand cattle. She stamped her foot. "Damn! I need to talk to you. Come home."

The clock in the parlor chimed for the half-hour. She looked around the corner to see it was six-thirty.

She poured herself a cup of coffee from the pot Frank had left simmering—something he always did. She pulled her wrapper tighter and tied the sash, and after opening the back door, she stepped onto the porch. The earthy smells of the ranch greeted her, the aroma of fresh hay and honeysuckle comingled with dust and barnyard odors. Lost in thought, she walked to the railing and gazed at the variegated colors of the morning sky. She considered the advantages of the Rocking C: peace and quiet, no horns, no sirens, no traffic. A pain stabbed at her heart. No David.

* * * *

After dressing and tidying up her bedroom, Taylor poured a second cup of coffee and went back outside to sit on the porch and wait for Frank to return. She needed to confirm her suspicion about lightning.

Her coffee, bitter from sitting, no longer tasted good and her stomach rumbled from hunger. She went back into the house to find something to eat, but after searching the pantry, came up empty-handed. How she missed munching on junk food like potato chips and cookies. She recalled Frank's comments about having to do all the cooking. She cupped her chin.

Hmm, maybe I'll surprise Mr. Cassidy with a hot lunch when he comes home.

Taylor tied an apron around her waist and picked through the pantry until she found preserved vegetables in a jar and some dried meat. She picked out two big potatoes and a large onion from the bin beneath the shelves, and with arms full, carried them to the table and laid them out before her. She had meat, vegetables, potatoes and an onion. What could she do with them? Make a stew?

Can I make a stew? Sure, you can make a stew, Taylor!

She opened the heavy oven door to find a pot, but instead found nothing. Then she remembered seeing one or two hanging on the back pantry wall. Finding one the right size, she brought it back to the table. Now she needed a knife. Where would she find one sharp enough? She looked around. "No drawers? Now stupid is that? Back to the pantry I go."

So this is where you keep things when you don't have drawers.

She stood for a moment to think of what else she might need. Nothing came to mind so she took her knife back to the table. She stood back with hands on her hips and prioritized her tasks. "Okay, knife to peel potatoes, onion and cut up meat. I need to open the jar. Hmm, I can do that. Then I'm going to mix everything together, and put them on to cook. Easy!"

Starting to peel the potatoes, Taylor realized she wasn't accustomed to using a knife. On the rare occasion she peeled anything, she used an actual potato peeler. She struggled to keep her thumb out of the way of the sharp blade, and although it took quite a while to finish, she managed. Pondering its odd composition, she attacked the onion. She'd never like onions and avoided them. Now she knew why. Layers… they were nothing but layers. When she finished the onion was much small than when she started and she could barely see to dice up the meat.

She wiped her eyes. "Damn, no wonder these give people bad breath."

With everything cut into bite-sized pieces, Taylor picked up the jar of preserved vegetables and surveyed the contents and mumbled, "What the heck is in here? I see tomatoes, but what are those green chunks?" She decided to use it regardless. "What difference does it make? I'm sure they're only vegetables, and after all, this is a stew."

She tried with all her might to open the jar, wishing for hot water to run over the top to loosen it, but instead, scurried back to the pantry and looked for something to help.

No can opener to pry with, no rubber sticky jar opener thing. Let's see. Hmm, when my mom couldn't open something, she pounded on it with a knife handle. I'll try that.

Luckily her mom's solution worked. She removed the lid and added the contents of the jar to the other ingredients, then added a dash of pepper and salt for taste. Carrying the full pot to the stove, she set the heavy container on a burner then realized she didn't know how to light it.

Using a towel, she lifted the coffeepot off the back burner. Carefully peaking underneath, she saw the remaining embers of burning wood.

Aha! Add wood, light and cook

She looked around the side of the stove and found a box filled with small pieces of wood and kindling. After lifting the burner, she added pieces to the tray, struck a match and started a fire.

Pleased with herself, she put the cover on the kettle then wiped the counter clean. She dried her hands on her apron then reached around and untied it, and hung it back on its hook. She stood back for a moment and reflected on her success.

"Let's see, lunch is cooking so what do I do now? Take in a matinee? Watch a soap opera?"

She compared Mariah's kitchen to her own and laughed. If only she'd gone to school to become an engineer instead of an attorney, she could make tons of money inventing things she knew already existed.

CHAPTER TWENTY-EIGHT

Denver, Colorado—2002

Mariah walked with David down the familiar hallway to Dr. Ramone's office. They arrived on time and were ushered in by the same cheery receptionist who'd previously greeted them. Dr. Ramone wasn't in the office yet, so Mariah and David instinctively sat in the same places they had before. Mariah folded her hands in her lap and took a deep breath. "I wonder what's going to happen today."

David checked his wristwatch. "Nothing unless the doctor gets here. She's late."

No sooner had he finished the sentence than Dr. Ramone hustled through the door, still buttoning her white lab coat.

"Sorry. I got held up in traffic." She sounded breathless. "Let's get started, shall we? Mariah, please take your place on the couch?" Dr. Ramone sat and took a moment to flip through her notes.

Mariah reclined on the sofa, both hands clasped across her stomach, hoping to quell the nervous feeling churning there.

Dr. Ramone, poised with pen in hand. "Mariah, you're going to feel yourself relaxing." She spoke in soft, dulcet tones. "I want you to listen to my voice and follow my instructions. Breathe deeply—in, out, in, out. Feel limpness drifting upward from your toes, spreading throughout your body. When I count to three, I want you to close your eyes. Feel them getting heavy… heavy… heavy. One, two, three."

Mariah sensed her body reacting to the doctor's voice like candle wax melting in the summer sun. Her chest rose and fell with each gentle breath, but try as she might, her eyes refused to open.

"Ready, Mariah. Now, we're traveling back in time. Going back to where we left off. See the years rolling back… back… back. We've stopped. It's 1872 and you're on your way to town with your husband and children. Can you see your family?"

"Yes, I see them." Cheery warmth embraced her and her lips curled into a smile.

"Can you tell me where you are?" Dr. Ramone asked.

"We're enjoying the ride into town. Jacob and Callie are bickering again. Stop it, you two. I don't want to listen to you all the way to town." Her smile vanished and she sensed tension across her brow. "The horses… the horses won't stop. We're going too fast. Make them stop, Frank."

Mariah's heart raced.

"Frank, please do something. Oh my God, I'm falling. Help me." Her body turned rigid. She visualized the sky, then total darkness.

Dr. Ramone patted Mariah's arm. "There, there. You're safe. Nothing can hurt you. Relax! Feel the calmness around you. Take a deep breath and let's go to the point where you feel like you're falling. Tell me what you see."

Mariah curled into a ball. Her hands formed fists under her chin. "Nothing. I don't see anything. It's dark and I hear Frank's voice, but I can't answer."

"Listen carefully. Frank calls to you, but is there anything else you hear? Concentrate, Mariah."

Squeezing her eyes together and drawing her knees to her chest, Mariah tried to hear anything other than Frank's voice. "He's calling me—Mariah, answer me, Mariah!"

She stiffened. "It's dark. I can't see anything, but I hear it! A noise! A loud noise." Her body jerked. "Now I see a light... a blinding flash. It's there then it's gone."

"Relax, Mariah. Feel your body sink into the cushions. Take a deep breath and let it out slowly. When I count to three, you're going to open your eyes and remember everything we talked about. You will feel totally relaxed and unafraid. One... two... three!"

Slowly, Mariah opened her eyes and stared at the ceiling. Everything was still fresh in her mind. If only she could make sense of it. Confused, she sat and swiveled to face the doctor. "Dr. Ramone, what do you think it all meant?"

The psychotherapist finished jotting notes and put her pad aside. "Let's talk about it and see if we can figure it out. First, you're in a state of darkness. I would say whatever happened in the accident rendered you unconscious."

His eyes wide, David interrupted. "That was an amazing thing to watch, but if someone's unconscious, can they still see light? What about the one Mariah saw?"

"What would cause a bright light on an open prairie in the daytime?" Dr. Ramone challenged him for an answer.

He pondered for a moment. "The sun?"

Dr. Ramone turned to look at Mariah. "Didn't you say you heard a loud noise?"

Mariah nodded. "Yes, very loud."

David snapped his fingers. "I've got it! Thunder and lightning. Thunder would make the noise and lightning would flash in the darkness. Exactly what Mariah said happened."

The doctor nodded. "That's one theory. Anything

else?"

He shrugged. "Nothing else comes to mind."

Mariah's neck tired of turning from David to the doctor, and she grew impatient for a solution. "I had to be unconscious," she cut in, "because I don't remember how I got to the hospital… how I woke up in this century. Until today, I didn't recall hearing anything, but now I keep hearing it over and over in my head. It had to be a clap of thunder before the lightning strike. Could this be the answer?"

Dr. Ramone stared blankly ahead for a moment, massaging her top lip. "Possibly. Lightning causes static electricity, and static has been known to move objects. It *is* quite possible—although I wouldn't want to share this outside this room—that the static electricity created some sort of time-warp phenomena."

CHAPTER TWENTY-NINE

Colorado Territory—1872

Taylor wiped a bead of sweat from her brow. She stood with arms folded and surveyed the results of her labor. The wooden floors were spotless, the furniture, dust-free, and clean clothes filled the basket in the corner. Beaming, she stood back and admired her accomplishments. "Well, Taylor, see you can be domestic. I wouldn't want to do it every day, but I have to admit, it does feel pretty rewarding. Won't Mr. Cassidy be shocked?"

Mentioning his name made her wonder where he was. He'd been gone all day and the stew intended for lunch still simmered on the stove. If he didn't show up soon, the delicious meal she'd prepared might well be ruined.

Crossing to the stove, she lifted the pot lid and stirred her masterpiece. She leaned into the rising mist to savor the aroma. Her nose wrinkled and she straightened. She bent to take another sniff. "Probably just needs more salt and pepper."

She picked up the shakers and liberally seasoned the stew, then replaced the lid. "There, I'll bet that's exactly what it needed." She had no doubt she'd created something worthy of a top-notch chef.

* * * *

Taylor heard loud laughter before Frank and the ranch

hands even passed under the big "C" on the gate. She wondered what they laughed about, but considered how men told tall tales and lies to one another. Working with a predominantly male staff had taught her well. How many times had she heard them swapping stories about their sexual conquests? She shivered as her night of passion with Frank flashed in her mind. She hoped he wasn't sharing anything about her.

He'd see to his horse before he came inside, but she struggled to justify her eagerness at his return. "He's Home?" Home? She covered her mouth.

She'd actually thought of this place as home! *Taylor, don't do this. This isn't your home and he isn't your husband. He's a good friend and nothing more.*

She busied herself setting the table. Of course he was a good friend, and she was anxious for him to taste her grand stew. That explained her strange emotions. Silly her for thinking it something more. She turned and fixed a smile on her face when the door opened.

Frank stomped the dust from his boots before he entered. As usual, he also slapped his hat against his pant leg. How strange, she predicted his actions beforehand. It was obvious he'd worked hard. A layer of gray dust covered his face and clothing. When he smiled, his pearly white teeth appeared from a dirt mask. "Evenin'."

Taylor laughed, holding her stomach and pointing. "Oh, you should see yourself. You look ridiculous. I couldn't tell it was you until you smiled."

He assumed an indignant stance. "Well it's hard to stay clean when you're wrestling with steers all day."

"Don't be a spoil sport. I was only kidding. And please, don't track all that dirt in here." She held up her hands and wiggled her fingers. "I've worked these to the bone today."

Frank didn't move, but he did glance around the room. "Oh lordy, she cleaned."

With hands on her hips, she cocked her head. "Yes, I did. And, what's more, I made you dinner… actually lunch, but…."

His head whipped around, and he looked at the steam rising from the kettle on the stove "Is that what I smell?" he asked.

She arched her brow. "I hope you mean that in a positive way."

"Let me try that again. What is that wonderful aroma I smell?" His words were sweet but lacked enthusiasm.

"That's much better." She smiled. "I'm anxious for you to taste what I've made, but you need a bath first. Take your clothes off right there—"

"I'd be happy to," he said as a wide smile crept across his face, "but I thought you wanted me to go up and take a bath. Make up your mind. Am I going to bathe, then eat or do you just want to see me nekked?"

"No, I do *not* want to see you 'nekked', but I do want you to take those filthy clothes off before you track dirt everywhere. I wasn't planning on watching. Just drop them and leave. I'll go out and get some water for the tub."

"Well, if I drop them and leave, then you have to bring the water upstairs, and by that time, I will be nekked. How do you plan to avoid seein' me then?" Clearly he took delight in teasing her.

Taylor grabbed both sides of her hair and yanked. "You are so frustrating some times."

She went into the pantry to get the bucket and reappeared. "Here's the plan," she said in a calm and slow fashion. "I will go outside and get water. While I'm doing that, you take off your dirty clothes and scoot upstairs. I suppose while you're waiting for the water you might want to get some clean clothes. A towel, perhaps. When the water is heated, I will bring it upstairs and leave it outside the door. I'll knock to let you know it's there, then leave. You open the door, pour the water in the tub, and take a bath. If you would like two buckets, we'll repeat the process. Clear enough?" As she walked out the backdoor, with bucket in hand, she looked over her shoulder and added, "And while his majesty is in the bath, I'll dish up his supper."

* * * *

Frank came downstairs, feeling clean and refreshed. At the stove, Taylor ladled something into a bowl. He sat at the table and waited, for what he wasn't sure. "I'm so hungry I could eat the hide off a cow."

She carried the bowl to the table and placed it before him like it was a prize he'd just won. Leaning over the spiraling steam, he inhaled. "Smells... interestin'."

Taylor filled her bowl and sat across from him. Instead of taking a taste, she sat, grinning, obviously waiting for him to sample the fare. He smiled and picked up his spoon, warily eyeing the bowl's contents. He paused for a moment and eyed the somewhat greenish-looking concoction, before he tasted and swallowed. Not wanting to offend her, he quickly took another huge bite.

A path of fire seared his tongue and burned down his throat. His eyes felt like they would blow out of their sockets. He blinked, hoping they wouldn't and tried to tough out the pain, but couldn't. He pushed back from the table so quickly his chair skidded backwards and toppled. He ran to the water pitcher, picked it up and chugged the cooling liquid until it was gone.

Turning around, he clutched his throat. "What's in that…?"

"Stew." A frown formed on Taylor's face. "It's only stew."

"What kind of *stew*?"

She pushed her bowl away. "Why? Is it bad?"

He shook his head. "I couldn't tell ya. I didn't have a chance to taste it. I think it burned out my taste buds. What's in it? Liquid fire?"

She hung her head. "Vegetables. There's onion, potato, some dried meat, and a jar of mixed vegetables I found in the pantry." She looked up, a frown tugging at her lips.

"Mixed vegetables? We don't have any mixed vegetables."

"Yes you do." There were two jars, but I only used one."

"Show me the other jar."

She crossed to the pantry and came out holding a small container. "This one."

Frank threw his head back and roared with laugher.

Taylor's bottom lip quivered. "I'm happy you find my attempt to surprise you so amusing."

He composed himself. "I truly appreciate all your effort, but sweetheart, those aren't mixed vegetables. That's pure jalapeño relish!"

Taylor's eyes welled, but she glared at him. "Well, I'm so sorry I couldn't read that invisible label on it. I thought I was doing something nice, but I guess I was wrong." She spun around and dashed up the stairs.

* * * *

Taylor sat on the edge of the bed and fumed. She was mad at herself for trying to impress Frank with her cooking skills when she didn't have any.

"*How* dare he laugh at me! That's the last time I'll cook anything for him," she muttered.

After thinking for a moment, she added, "That's probably just fine with him."

She suddenly realized she'd forgotten to tell Frank the very thing she had waited all day to tell him, but she was far too mad to approach him now.

A small tap sounded on the door. "I'm sorry." Frank's voice came from the other side. "I didn't mean to upset you. I really do appreciate what you did today. Your stew would have been delicious if only... Well, your stew would have been delicious, I know. You're probably too mad to talk, so I'm not going to bother you. But, I have a surprise for you tomorrow, so sleep well."

What surprise?

Suddenly her thoughts became words. "What surprise?" she called out.

"I'm taking you on a horseback ride tomorrow."

Before his words had a chance to sink in, she heard his bedroom door close. Reality dawned on her and she gasped. "That's not a surprise, that's... that's a threat."

She went to the armoire and changed into her nightgown. Still fuming, she pulled back the quilt and climbed into bed, and slammed her fist into her pillow. "Horseback ride?" she grumbled. "Maybe when hell freezes over!"

CHAPTER THIRTY

Denver, Colorado—2002

David and Mariah left Dr. Ramone's office with doubts about a third appointment. As he pulled out of the parking garage, Mariah stared vacantly out the car window at the people strolling along the sidewalk. She wondered if any of them were visitors from another era.

She turned to David. "Now I'm even more confused and frustrated. Dr. Ramone believes I might be here because of something called a time warp, but I got the feeling she doesn't know of another single soul who's had the same misfortune. So, if we figured out the problem, what's the solution?"

He sighed loudly, and reached over to turn off the radio. "I don't know. Time warps are something they make movies of or write about in books. I always thought it was just a bunch of baloney."

"Do you still feel that way?"

"I'm not even sure how I feel. Everything you said under hypnosis reinforces the fact that you aren't Taylor. Even if I consider you might be, why would a head trauma make you remember a whole other life? There has to be an explanation, and after today, I'm convinced you are who you say you are."

She sank into the softness of the seat and sighed. "Thanks for finally believing me, but even if you do, nothing changes the fact I'm still stranded in 2002. The family I love and want to be with is back in 1872. How am I going to get home?"

David glanced over at her. His brow furrowed over saddened eyes. "I don't know Mariah. I wish I did. I'm not even sure what good seeing Dr. Ramone again will do. She can't create magic."

Mariah released a breath through pursed lips. "Maybe I should have another accident and hit my head again."

"Don't say things like that. Don't even think them." His grip tightened on the steering wheel.

"I feel so helpless. All I want to do is go home."

"I know. I want Taylor back, too. Now that I know you're Mariah, I'm really worried about what happened to my wife. Are you in that body all alone or do you feel like you have company?"

The idea of sharing a body sent a shiver down her spine. "Ugh, that's a horrible thing to even think about. As far as I know, I'm all alone."

"Well, if you're here, then wouldn't it stand to reason Taylor is where you're supposed to be?"

Mariah hadn't even thought of that. "Oh, my gosh. You may be right. Taylor is with Frank and my kids. Now I have something else to worry and wonder about."

He chuckled. "Can you imagine what Frank must be going through? Remember how I described Taylor? Oh the poor man. It wouldn't be so bad, if he had known her from the beginning, but..."

Mariah didn't see the humor in Frank being with another woman. "Aren't you even the least bit worried?"

"Of course, I am. Until now I believed you *were* Taylor but there isn't a whole lot I can do to change things. Rather than fall apart, I prefer to think she's at least somewhere safe.

After hearing all you've said about Frank, it doesn't sound like he'd harm her in any way."

"He's a wonderful man." She sighed. "I'm sure Taylor's safe and sound, but I wonder about Frank. If your wife is as independent and stubborn as you say, I think she may have met her match."

David fell silent and Mariah tried to apply all the things he'd told her about Taylor to the picture in her mind. All of a sudden, she remembered his description of his wife's sexual appetite, and the hair on the back of her neck bristled. She chewed her bottom lip and stared vacantly through the windshield.

She didn't realize they were home until David drove into the garage and closed the door. As he reached to turn off the key, she turned to him. "Do you think they've been intimate?"

David's eyes widened. "I haven't gotten that far in my thinking process, but now that you pose the question..." He rubbed his chin. "If Taylor is with Frank, they've been together as long as we have. I told you she is a very sexual being. If I had to wager a guess, it would have to be yes."

The thought of someone else in Frank's arms stabbed her Mariah's heart. "Doesn't that bother you?"

"Of course it does. But if they've made love, I think I understand why."

"How *can* you understand?" She stiffened and blinked back tears.

"Why *can't* you?"

"What do you mean?" The timed garage light clicked off and they were left in the dark. Although David sat next to her, he was barely visible. "Remember how I explained my feelings about you the night I came to your room? You look like Taylor, you walk like her, you feel like her, and I love my wife. I didn't want to believe you weren't her. I tried to do what came naturally to me, although not as frequently as Taylor would like… I wanted to make love to my wife."

Mariah thought about what he said. If Taylor looked like the woman Frank supposed was Mariah, and knowing how much he enjoyed making love, then it would certainly stand to reason they'd shared a bed. "I see what you mean, but that doesn't make me feel any better. As a matter of fact, I don't like it one bit. I've managed to stay true."

"Mariah, don't fret about it. It won't change anything. If we're lucky, they're at the same stage we are. Frank most certainly has noticed a drastic change in your behavior… or Taylor's. I'm sure he's figured something isn't right."

When David opened his door, the car's dim interior light seemed harsh compared to the darkness. Mariah blinked. "Maybe you're right. Taylor and I certainly don't sound anything alike."

"Boy, you can say that again," he mumbled as he stepped out.

* * * *

Mariah finished loading the dishwasher, added the soap, and closed the door. She stood at the sink, wiping the counter, when she glanced out the window. Her gaze jerked back to the strange sight and she screamed. "David!"

He raced into the kitchen. "What! What's wrong?"

She swallowed hard and pointed out the window. "Wha…what's that?"

He glanced through the glass. "What's what? I don't see anything."

"In the sky. What's that in the sky?" Her voice trembled.

David craned his neck to look up. He pointed to the object. "That? That's an airplane."

* * * *

As Mariah readied for bed, she still tried to understand David's explanation of the flying machine. He sounded so casual when he told how it soared like a bird and carried people from place to place.

She shimmied her nightgown down the length of her body, then stopped and shook her head. "How in the world? What keeps this… this airplane in the sky? And it takes people from one place to another?"

A sudden thought occurred to her. Maybe it could carry her back home.

CHAPTER THIRTY-ONE

Colorado Territory—1872

Frank rapped on Taylor's door. "Get up. It's time to go ridin'."

She forced her eyes open and wondered if she was dreaming. She listened for a minute.

Another knock. "Taylor, C'mon, wake up." And Frank's voice.

She rolled over and stuck her tongue out at the closed door, then swiped at her half-lidded eyes. "What time is it?" she groaned.

"It's six-thirty. We don't want to wait until the hottest part of the day." He cracked the door open and peeked around it. I don't know if you've found it yet, but Mariah keeps a split skirt in the armoire, and make sure to wear boots."

Taylor sighed. "Frank, I don't even know how to ride a horse. The only time I've ever been around one was when we went to town in the buggy."

"It's easy. There's nothin' to it. You'll enjoy it. So get up and get dressed! I've got coffee ready downstairs."

Begrudgingly, she threw back the covers and sat on the edge of the bed. She took a deep breath and pursed her lips into a pout. "I don't want to go horseback riding."

Downstairs, Frank called her name.

"Oh, for God's sake. Give me a minute," she muttered.

She rummaged through the armoire and found Mariah's skirt. It was brown suede with fringe along the sides.

Gee, this looks charming. I shudder to imagine what I'm supposed to wear on the top. She searched again until she found a plain, white blouse, and felt satisfied. At least it wasn't as horrid as what she expected to find.

****

Taylor descended the stairs and walked into the kitchen. "Well, here I am. Annie friggin' Oakley."

Frank poured a cup of coffee and handed it to her. "You look very nice."

"Well, I do have to admit it's more like what I'm used to. Certainly better than those period costumes I've been forced to wear. Did you know, I actually tried on your jeans one day? If they had fit, I'd have worn them everyday. I'm a jeans-and-tee-shirt kind of girl on the weekend. I dress for power the rest of the week."

He finished a sip of his own coffee. "I have no idea what you just said… bout that dressin' for power, but I had a hard time getting Mariah to even try a split skirt. I saw them in the catalog and wanted her to buy one. She thought it downright immoral for a woman to wear pants. But that was a while back. Now, she's glad now she has them. It sure makes ridin' easier."

He isn't giving up. "Do we really have to do this?"

"C'mon, finish your coffee. I packed a little snack. We'll ride out to a place I know and have a bite to eat." He grabbed his hat off the rack and pushed it firmly down on his head.

She slumped along behind him, scuffing her toes in

the dust. "I don't even like horses," she mumbled. "They smell bad and are way too big."

It was apparent nothing she said affected him. He had two saddled horses waiting in the barn. She wasn't at all pleased when he pointed out the one she was to ride. It seemed much taller and wider than Gert, and Taylor remembered the ominous look she'd gotten from the old mare on the day of the social. Suddenly, Taylor felt very intimidated, something she not at all used to.

Frank untied the reins of his own horse. "Watch me. I'll give you a little lesson."

She rolled her eyes. "Great."

He held the saddle horn with his left hand and put his left foot in the stirrup. Pulling himself up, he threw his right leg over the horse's back. Once in the saddle, he picked up the reins and peered down at her. "See how easy?"

"Easy for you."

"You can do it, too. Once you're in the saddle, use the reins to tell the horse what you want her to do."

"I can tell her from here. I want someone else to go on this silly ride." She looked up and smiled sweetly.

He ignored her sarcasm. "Whatever way you pull the reins, that's the direction the horse will go. If you want to move, just nudge her sides with your feet, and when you want to stop, pull back!" He dismounted. "Okay. Now, you try."

"If I must." She exhaled a loud breath.

Frank untied her horse and positioned it next to her. "Now, just like I showed you. Left hand on the saddle horn, foot in the stirrup."

Taylor firmly grasped the horn. She hoisted her leg, trying to fit her boot into the stirrup. She looked over her shoulder at Frank. "That last time I had my foot in a stirrup, I had a pap smear. This looks like its going to be about as much fun."

Frank gave her a quizzical look but said nothing.

She tried to pull herself up, but fell backwards.

"That's okay. Try it again," he reassured.

After the fifth try, Frank apparently realized she lacked the necessary skills. While she held the saddle horn, he put her foot in the stirrup, then placed his palms under her buttocks and hefted her into the saddle. She clutched the horn tightly and adjusted her position. Searching for the other stirrup, she managed to fit her boot snugly inside then picked up the reins. "Thanks…I think." Her heart thudded. "Okay, now what?" She dreaded the answer.

Frank mounted his black stallion and headed it toward the door. "Just follow me and relax."

"You've gotta be kidding. You do that in a bed or a chair, but here?" She gave the reins a tug to the left. The horse turned its head and stared at her, but didn't move. She felt certain she saw anger, or at least a bad attitude. "Frank," she called in a lowered voice. "I don't think this horse likes me."

"Taylor, calm down. Powder is a gentle mare my daughter rides all the time. Don't be scared. You just have to show her you're the boss."

"Okay, horsey. I'm the boss. Let's not forget that." Taylor closed her eyes and yanked hard on the reins, not feeling in control at all. Sensing movement, she opened her eyes to discover the mare had turned and followed Frank's stallion. Taylor shifted her rear end from side to side, trying to find a comfort zone with the plodding movement. She flexed her knees, lifted out of the saddle then sat back down. She dared not speak for fear of scaring the horse.

As the exited the barn, Frank glanced around. "How

are you doing?"

"F-fine," she whispered.

Outside, he stopped and waited until she caught up. "We'll take it slow. There's no hurry. All you have to do is let her have her head and she'll do the work."

"Have her head? What in the hel...ah, heck does that mean?"

"That means leave slack in the reins. You only need to guide her when you want to go left, right, or stop."

"So, she knows where we're going and I don't?"

"She'll just walk alongside ol' Rebel here and go wherever he goes. I think Powder likes him."

"Swell."

* * * *

Taylor started to relax and developed a rhythm with the horse. She smiled over at Frank. "This isn't as awful as I thought would be."

"See, I told you you'd like it," he said.

"I didn't say I like it. I said it isn't quite as bad as I expected."

"Well, let's hope we don't run into any more rain."

Rain!

The word stirred a memory. "How could I have forgotten? You just reminded me of something important. When we talked about the lightning strike that happened the day of Mariah's accident, I didn't connect it to myself. But yesterday, when I was drying off after my bath, I remembered. Static electricity! Lightning is a sort of static, isn't it?"

"I don't reckon I even know the meaning of that word. But what does drying off have to do with lightning?"

"I remembered back to when I was driving to work, it started to rain pretty hard, and there must have been a lot of static in the air because it kept interfering with my radio."

He rolled his eyes. "I have to ask. What's a radio?"

"I'll explain another time. The important thing is that something to do with electricity happened the day of my accident, too. Do you think there could be a connection?"

"I wish I knew. I don't know much about electricity, or lightning for that fact. But it sure makes you wonder. If this is a clue, what do we do with it?"

She shook her head. "I don't know. I was hoping you would."

Frank didn't say anything, just leaned back in the saddle. He pushed his hat higher on his head and allowed a dark curl to fall forward. Taylor fought the urge to reach across and push it aside. For a fleeting moment, looking at his handsome profile, she envied Mariah.

* * * *

Taylor reined the mare to a halt next to the corral. Just as she had when they stopped to eat, she removed her right foot from the stirrup, pulled it up and back over the saddle. She wasn't very graceful, but she did manage to clear leather and land standing up this time. "Boy, am I glad that adventure is over."

Frank had already dismounted and stooped to pick up her reins where she'd dropped them. "Are you gonna tell me you didn't have a good time?"

She laughed. "All right, so I did enjoy myself. And it wasn't as scary as I thought, although I still don't like the way Powder looks at me. From the way my thighs and butt feel, I imagine this is something you have to get used to." She rubbed her backside with both hands.

He grinned. "I guess I should have told you it might cause some irritation."

"At least, now I know I'm not the only pain in the butt around here." She laughed and waddled back toward the house.

CHAPTER THIRTY-TWO

Denver, Colorado—2002

Mariah and David sat at the breakfast table. They ate in silence until he dropped his fork into his empty plate and scooted back from the table, dabbing his lips with a napkin. "Mariah, I'm going back to work on Monday. I have to. We can't afford for me to be off any longer, especially since you aren't working… I mean since Taylor isn't working. Today's Saturday and we still have two days until I get back in the trenches, so while you were in the shower, I called and arranged something fun for us to do today."

She clucked her tongue against the back of teeth. "I knew you'd eventually have to return to whatever it is you do, but I'm not sure how I feel about it. I'm going to be all alone for the first time." She decided not to dwell on something she couldn't change. "So, just what fun thing have you arranged?"

"A friend I work with knows a guy who runs a small tourist enterprise. I've never met Garrett personally, but…"

She shrugged and flashed him a confused look. "Tourist enterprise? What exactly is that?"

"People pay him to fly…"

Before he finished his sentence, she realized where he was leading. Her eyes bulged in disbelief. "Fly? As in an airplane? Don't tell me you expect me to get in one of those… those flying contraptions."

"Come on. People fly every day. It'll be fun. Trust me."

"Where I'm from people do not fly. Birds do."

"Where's your pioneer spirit? I thought people from 1872 had grit. If everyone felt like you do, we *wouldn't be* flying today."

His inference insulted her. She straightened in her chair. "I *do* have grit! You have no idea how easy you have it today. You wouldn't last a month in 1872. You and your TV, your recliner, your swimming pool, your dishwasher, your garage door opener. You have no idea what grit is."

He nodded. "Maybe you're right. Maybe grit wasn't the word I was looking for. How about 'adventuresome spirit'? Don't you trust me?"

"What has trust got to do with anything?"

"I wouldn't plan anything that would harm you. I've flown thousands of time. Just think about what you'll have to tell your kids when you get home."

Mariah turned solemn; her shoulders sagged. "If I ever *get* home."

* * * *

As they walked toward the 'jet' David jabbered. Mariah wondered how she let herself get talked into flying. Her heart hammered as if trying to beat its way right through her chest. The closer they came, the more the urge to turn and run appealed to her. It was as if David sensed her thoughts and held her hand a little tighter. As they neared, her stomach twisted and turned. She needed reassurance. "David, are you sure this safe? I realize we haven't figured out how I'm going to get home, but I would at least like to stay alive to try."

He chuckled. "Haven't we already had this discussion? You're perfectly safe. Garrett is a licensed pilot. He flies all the time. People pay him to fly them to wherever they need to go. It's what he does."

"Well, I've already survived riding in a car, and none of those new-fangled gadgets in your house have killed me, so I'll go, but I don't have to like it."

"Well, if you don't like it, I won't ever make you go again. I'm going to be right beside you, so it's not like you're going alone."

"That would assure me, but Frank was beside me the day I ended up here."

They walked the rest of the way in silence.

Garrett was already inside the 'plane' and smiled out the window at them. At first glimpse, the slivers of gray marking his brown hair made him appear older than David. His gentle eyes and kind smile quelled her fears momentarily. She surveyed the strange configuration of the airplane. It seemed much larger than it appeared from a distance.

David stood next to the door and motioned for her to enter, but her feet were frozen to the ground. She understood why Frank's old mare dug in her heels when he buckled her to the plow. She didn't any part of what was planned for her.

"Go ahead, Mariah, get in." David coaxed.

She took a deep breath, forced herself to put one foot in front of the other and ducked inside. Visions of confinement in the elevator ran through her mind, and she took a deep breath.

Next to Garrett a seat was vacant, and four more empty ones sat behind him. Mariah moved directly across and sat. Garrett turned and smiled at her again. She tried to mask her fear and smiled back at him.

David stooped to enter, closed the door and sat next to her. "Fasten your seat belt."

She heard his click. Securing her own belt, she swallowed hard.

He reached out and touched her arm. "Are you okay?"

She nodded because a lump choked off her words.

He made introductions. "Garrett, this is Mariah. Mariah, this is Garrett."

Again Garrett smiled and nodded, but quickly turned his attention to the numerous knobs and dials in front of him. A roaring noise caused Mariah to jump. Her knuckles whitened as she gripped the arms of her seat. Compared to the car, the plane sounded deafening. She covered her ears. "Why is it so loud?" she yelled over the din.

He leaned closer. "It's noisier at the beginning. He has to test the jets and make sure everything is okay. It won't be this loud all the time."

Just as he finished his sentence, the racket lessened. She folded her hands in her lap, grasping her fingers, and managed a quick grin. "That's much better."

When the plane started moving, Mariah tensed and leaned back against her seat. She grabbed David's hand. Faster, faster the plane maneuvered along the narrow strip until the wheels left the ground. The force exerted against her body held her prisoner against the seat.

Finally, she peered out the window, still clutching David's hand. She watched the distance between the airplane and the ground increase as the aircraft climbed higher. Holding her breath, she forced herself to look forward, her head firmly planted against the headrest. Through the windshield, she glimpsed only blue sky.

She turned to find David smiling at her. "Can I have my hand back now? My fingers are numb."

Mariah realized she needed to breathe. She released

her pent-up breath and released his hand. "Sorry!"

"See, that wasn't so bad. Garrett is leveling off now so you can just sit back and take in the sights."

She swallowed and turned to look out the window. Craning her neck to peek over the edge, she looked down. "Oh, heavenly days."

The landscape resembled the patchwork quilt on her bed at home. Colors of the rainbow seemed to have fallen to earth. For as far as she could see, the backdrop was nothing but blue sky and white clouds. It was no wonder birds chose to fly. Amazement replaced her fear.

She pressed closer to the window and gazed down. "What are those little things moving down there?"

David leaned across and looked. "Those are cars on the interstate."

"They look more like ants." She giggled.

The immensity of space dwarfed the tall buildings that had once awed her, and the distant mountain peaks, still covered with an icing of snow, appeared close enough to touch. She was speechless at the beauty that lay before her. Never in her wildest dreams did she ever think she would fly.

CHAPTER THIRTY-THREE

Colorado Territory—1872

Frank spent more and more time working out on the range. With a ranch to run, he couldn't continue to ignore his responsibilities. Taylor almost wished the kids were around so she'd have some company. This morning, she almost asked if she could go with him, but chose solitude over horseback riding again.

Being alone gave her too much time to think about David and how much she missed him. She and Frank had already discussed the possibility that Mariah had assumed her role in modern-day Denver, so Taylor tried to picture how David would get along with the meek and mild woman Frank often described. Now that she'd been assured by men from two different centuries she wasn't the easiest person to live with, her confidence waned. She slammed the iron cover down on the stove. "What if he likes her better? What if…."

The sound of horses in the yard interrupted her ranting. The sun was already setting, and she welcomed the sound of Frank's voice calling goodnight to his men. She'd managed to prepare dinner because she knew he'd be tired, and had fried up a slice of ham and boiled some potatoes. It was something she'd watched him do, so it wasn't that difficult. This time, she tasted everything beforehand.

She turned from the stove when he walked in, and greeted him with a smile. "I thought you'd never get home.

You must be exhausted."

He hung his hat on the rack and sniffed the air. "Smells good in here. You've been cookin'?"

"At the risk of being insulted again, yes I have been. But I tasted it and it's safe this time."

Frank laughed, and bent to pull of his left boot. "I'm so hungry, I could eat jalapeño relish."

Her laughter blended with his as she stuck her finger into test the water heating on the back burner. "I can guarantee you this is not a repeat performance of that night." She pointed to the steaming pail. "I knew you'd want a bath before eating, so I have water ready for you. Would you like me to heat more?"

"Nope, one bucket's enough. I'm gonna get in, wash off the layer of dirt and get out. I'm starved."

* * * *

Frank finished the last bite and leaned back in his chair. "That was mighty delicious. Thanks."

Taylor smiled at his compliment. "It did taste good, even if I do say so myself."

She pushed her plate aside and leaned on the table. "Who knows, if I ever get to go home, maybe I'll start cooking for David more often."

Frank noticed the sadness in her eyes when she mentioned home. "He'd probably like that. We men like to be spoiled. I have to admit I'd sure like to have Mariah home. No offense, but she's about the best cook around. Besides, I really miss her."

"No offense taken. We both know my cooking skills are dismal at best. She's pretty lucky to have a man like you. If

I had met you under different circumstances and didn't love my own husband so much, I might try to give her a run for her money."

He winked. "I know what you mean. You're a fine and genuine person, Taylor, and you've come a long way since we met. Heck, I don't think I've heard you cuss in… gee, I can't even remember the last time."

"I've been trying to stop. From hearing you talk about Mariah all these nights, I've done a lot of comparison. Don't get me wrong. I'm fine with who I am, but there's always room for improvement. One thing is never going to change though…" She yanked a long lock of hair forward and wrinkled her nose. "I'll never get used to having red hair."

* * * *

Taylor pulled the curtains back and stared into the darkness. Frank had already gone to bed, but sleep wouldn't come for her. She pondered the events of the past weeks and wondered how David had spent the time. Her heart ached, longing to see him again. She willed her love for him to float up to the heavens and be delivered through the twinkling of a star. But she gazed up and saw no stars. The heavens were devoid of light much like her life without David.

Suddenly, the blanket of darkness came alive. On the far horizon, bolts of lightening illuminated the sky; resounding claps of thunder provided fanfare for the fantastic light display. The beauty of nature's fury mesmerized her and held her rapt at the window.

As the storm moved closer, a brilliant bolt lit up the entire bedroom. It seemed to penetrate the glass. Its sudden surge of power frightened her and she backed away. Her hands tingled. She wrung them together, wondering why they felt so weird.

The strange sensation slowly traveled up her arms and throughout the rest of her body. The room began to spin. She perched on the edge of the bed and waited, hoping the dizziness would pass. "What's wrong with me?" she mumbled.

Another clap of thunder resonated through the room. She leaned over and rested her head against the pillow. "I don't feel very well."

* * * *

Denver, Colorado--2002

Mariah pulled her vacant gaze from the television screen and checked the time on the clock over the mantle. The days since David had returned to work were long and lonely. Her only pastime had become TV, but that didn't fill all the many hours she had to think about Frank, Cassie and Jacob. She fought every day not to give up on the belief that one day she would go home again. Seeing it was almost time for David, she rose and meandered into the kitchen.

She so looked forward to him coming home every night, and always made sure he had a good dinner as a reward for his hard work. The time they spent talking was what she missed most. When she needed to stay strong, he'd always gave her hope. She checked on dinner and set the table.

The garage door opened and closed. She rushed to get the food served up, and eagerly waited for him to come inside. When he walked in, she ignored the slight fluttering in her stomach. He looked so handsome in his suit. She smiled at him. "Hi. How was your day?"

He loosened his tie. "Same old thing. Not bad, but not

as much fun as hanging around here with you."

"I miss your company, too. If I'm destined to stay here, I've got to find something to do. There's nothing to keep me busy here. You're too neat, and I don't have children to pick up after and scold. I get so lonely. You're the only person I know."

"Maybe we shouldn't have cancelled our last appointment with Dr. Ramone." David took off his sport coat, hung it on the back of the chair and went to the sink to wash his hands.

Mariah sat at the table. "No, I think we were right. There was nothing more she could do for us. We wanted an answer and we got one—just not the one I wanted."

She, as usual, waited until David filled his plate before filling her own. When he took a bite of his dinner, his eyes lit up. "Taste all right?" She asked.

"Yummy. Who wouldn't love fried chicken, crispy and brown?" He eagerly dug into his mashed potatoes.

"You act like you haven't eaten in a week."

He swallowed and laughed. "I keep thinking, one of these days you just might go home and I'll be forced to fend for myself again."

* * * *

After dinner, Mariah sat with David in the living room. He was immersed in watching *Cops* on television, while she was lost in thought. She sat on the sofa, legs folded under her, and stared through the sliding glass doors at the lights illuminating the swimming pool. It started to rain. Droplets gently pelted the still water of the pool sending ripples across the serene surface. How she wished she could find serenity. There was no peace from the haunting faces of her family—

those she loved and missed terribly.

A sudden clap of thunder startled her and sent a shiver racing through her body. She glanced at David, still engrossed in his program and oblivious to the noise. Lightening silhouetted the trees in the backyard as a brilliant bolt lit up the sky behind. Within a few seconds, she heard another roar of thunder and saw the rain's intensity increase. The pool water changed from gentle ripples to a frenzied display of dancing bubbles. Another bolt of lightning seared across the sky. The living room went dark.

Before she could ask what had happened, a clap of thunder shivered the plate glass doors as though they were nothing more than a muslin sheet; the vase sitting on the table next to her crashed to the floor.

Mariah heard David fumbling in the dark. Her body felt strange—prickly shocks surged through her hands and arms, and she suddenly became very lightheaded. She straightened her legs, put her feet on the floor and leaned back against the soft velour pillows of the couch. "David… there's a candle in—"

* * * *

David struck a match and put it to the wick of the candle. "Voilà, we have light!"

Not hearing a response, he glanced over at Mariah. "Are you asleep?"

She didn't answer.

He crossed to the couch and sat next to her. "Mariah, are you all right?" When she didn't respond, he gently tapped her cheek. "Wake up!"

Slowly, her eyelids opened. She squinted at first then

blinked several times; candlelight reflecting in chocolate pool. Her gaze roamed the dimly lit room then returned to him. She flattened her back against the sofa and blinked a few more times. "David?" Her tone held a definite question.

"Yes. Who else were you expecting?" He laughed.

"Oh, David! My God, is it really you?" She threw her arms around his neck and smothered his face with kisses. Pulling away, she studied his face then snaked her arms around him again." It's really you, David. It's really you," she crooned.

Her sudden show of affection perplexed him. He reached behind his head and unclasped her arms from around his neck, then holding her hands in his own, asked, "Mariah, did you have a bad dream or something?"

She lunged forward and covered his lips with a passionate kiss. Her probing tongue encouraged him to part his lips and allow her access. He complied, although with eyes wide open. Their tongues intertwined in a long overdue, but oh so familiar kiss.

David pulled away and held her at arm's length. "Taylor, is that you? I mean *really* you?"

She giggled with heartfelt delight. "Yes, my darling. It's me. I'm home! Finally."

* * * *

Colorado Territory—1872

Mariah rolled over to see the sun filtering into the room through the thin curtains. Minute dust particles floated in the rays, dancing until they disappeared from sight. She wondered how long she'd slept.

The bed seemed more comfortable than she remembered. She stroked the covers and fingered the intricate patchwork stitching. Her eyes widened. "It can't be."

She pulled the corner of the bedding up to her face.

My quilt! Lordy, it's the quilt Grandma made me.

Mariah bolted upright and scanned the room. Her gaze locked on her familiar washbowl and pitcher, the oval mirror on the wall. "Dear Lord, don't let this be a dream."

She ran to the armoire and threw open the doors. Her own familiar clothing greeted her. She pulled the hem of her cottony nightgown to her face. "It's mine…this is all mine. Thank you God, thank you, thank you, thank you."

She bolted through the bedroom door and sprinted into the hallway. "Frank, Frank," she screamed at the top of her lungs. "Where are you?"

When there was no response, she raced downstairs, her feet barely making contact. "Frank," she continued to shout. "Where are you?

Finding the kitchen empty, she hurried to the window and scanned the yard. At that very moment, he sauntered out of the barn. Her wonderfully handsome husband, Frank.

She burst through the door and onto the porch—her wonderful porch with climbing vines and rocking chairs. She paused to inhale the delicious aroma of honeysuckle for validation before she crossed the yard and bounded into her husband's arms. She sent his hat flying. "Frank, oh my darling Frank. It's me, Mariah. I'm home."

EPILOGUE

Taylor
Denver, Colorado—2002

A million thoughts ran through Taylor's mind. Had it been a dream or had it really happened? David slept next to her—she heard his gentle snores. She looked around for verification. Yes, she was in her own tastefully decorated bedroom.

But, what of Frank, the Rocking C and Colorado Territory? Everything seemed so confusing at the moment.

She reached out and gently touched David's backside for assurance he was real. She remembered making love last night. That certainly wasn't a dream. She still basked in the afterglow. Was everything else she remembered just a figment of her imagination? She pondered waking David and asking if anything strange had happened.

She rolled onto her back and pulled the blankets up.

Sure, wake him up and ask if you came home from 1872. If it was a dream, he's going to have you committed.

Maybe when he woke he would broach the subject, and then again, maybe not. She locked her hands behind her head, stared at the ceiling and replayed the dream: Handsome Frank Cassidy, the beautiful porch with the fragrant honeysuckle, the horseback ride she hated. It all seemed so vivid in her mind. And what about the church social? How in the world could she have dreamed that? She never went to church. A glance at the clock on the night stand showed the time was five thirty. What woke her so early? Usually she had to have an alarm. Was this a workday?

Oh my God, I don't even know what day it is. Matter of fact, I don't remember anything about work lately.

The last day she remembered had been Tuesday, but not in this era. She pulled the pillow over her face to stifle her groan of frustration.

Finally, she couldn't stand not knowing. She nudged David with her elbow. "Honey, wake up."

David moaned and pulled the sheet up over his head. The name "Mariah" crept into his mind. Memories of last night flashed in his head. Taylor, his beautiful Taylor had come back to him. Did Mariah go home to Frank? David thought a minute and wondered if it had just been a dream. Time travel... right!

Taylor elbowed him again. "Honey, I need to ask you a question, but I'm not even sure how to start."

He took the sheet away from his face. "This sounds serious." He had a few questions of his own, but wanted to hear hers first. "What time is it?" he asked, still groggy.

She sat and crossed her legs, Indian style. "It's early. I think I may have had a strange dream—"

Before she finished, he pulled her over on his chest. "I was just going to tell you the same thing. Did your dream have anything to do with someone named Mariah?"

Taylor swallowed. "You mean it wasn't a dream? It really happened?"

He cradled her in his arms. "I don't know what *it* was, nor do I have an explanation, but something happened all right. I got a phone call telling me you were in an accident on the way to work. I spent two weeks at your hospital bedside, but believe me, the person I brought home was not you. Somehow, last night, you came back to me."

He held her tight, afraid she'd disappear again.

Taylor took a deep breath and rose to her knees next to him. "Holy shit, then I'm home and everything is fine." A million thoughts swam in her head. "David, you have no idea what I've been through. I woke up in 1872 somewhere in Colorado. I've been with Frank, Mariah's husband. He wouldn't believe I wasn't Mariah—"

David put a finger against her lips and stopped her babbling. "You don't need to explain, Taylor. Trust me; I have a firsthand knowledge of what Frank went through. I'm sure Mariah wanted to kill me a few times while she was here."

Taylor held her head in her hands. "I have so much to tell you, I don't know where to start. It was amazing and awful at the same time." She took a deep breath. "Trying to convince everyone I wasn't Mariah... Do you know they didn't even have indoor plumbing? I wanted to call you, but every time I mentioned the phone, no one had a clue what I was talking about. I went to a church social in a buggy, I had to wear these awful, awful clothes, and I even rode a horse."

David snorted. "You... on a horse? I would have loved to have been there."

She gave him a shove. "You just wouldn't believe what it was like to live back then. I didn't have my makeup, I didn't have my cell phone, and oh my God, I had red hair...horrible, horrible red hair."

"And green eyes, I'll bet. The whole time Mariah was here, she looked just like you, but she knew she should have had red hair and green eyes."

It hadn't been a dream. Taylor tried to picture Frank's delight in getting his Mariah back. Would he remember his time with Taylor at all? She paused for a moment to think what 2002 must have been like for Mariah. She felt a strange bond with Frank's wife, although in reality they had never met. Taylor gazed at her husband. "I just thought about how Mariah must have felt. If I found 1872 so exasperating, she must have been amazed by what she found here."

The look on David's face indicated he recalled something pleasant. "It was like a little girl learning new things every day. Some days, I wanted to spank her for asking so many questions. It was frustrating at times." He shook his head. "Do you know, I actually made her fly?"

"Fly? Oh you didn't! She must have been terrified."

"At first, but once we got up in the air, she loved it. And you should have seen her in the kitchen. She couldn't believe her eyes!"

Jalapeño relish! Taylor chuckled to herself. "I know, I was pretty amazed in her kitchen, too."

She stretched out and snuggled next to David. For a moment neither spoke. Taylor never wanted to forget Frank. Being with him had changed her life for the better. Although he hadn't preached to her, he had taught her patience, understanding, and most importantly, devotion. His love for Mariah had helped Taylor see the importance of her own relationship with David, and the slow pace of the Rocking C had helped her learn to take one day at a time. Now that she was back, she vowed to spend time with David and do the simple, yet important, things like taking walks and enjoying cozy evenings together. She loved being married to him and planned to make sure he knew it. Rather than her job, she'd make David her life's priority.

His voice interrupted her thoughts. "I know we still have lots to talk about, but you don't want to be late for work."

She reached up and caressed his cheek then passed her fingers across his full lips. "We'll have lots of time to tell each other all about all the things that happened, but I'd rather spend the next half hour or so making up for some lost time. And, if I'm late for work, so what?"

Mariah
Colorado Territory—1872

When Mariah leapt at Frank, she almost bowled him over. He unclasped her hands from behind his neck, held them in his, and looked at her from beneath an arched brow. "Whoa, little lady. You're stronger than you look. What's got you so all fire excited this morning?"

Mariah noticed his curious look and took a breath. He acted as though she hadn't even been gone. Was it all a dream? She peered into his cobalt eyes. "I guess I'm just really glad to see you."

He picked up his hat and dusted it against his pant leg. "Well, I'm happy to see you, too."

She glanced around the yard. The barn, the bunkhouse, the porch—why did she feel like she'd missed it all so terribly? And her children? It seemed she hadn't seen Callie and Jacob in ages. She nibbled her bottom lip.

"Is something wrong?" Frank asked. "You have a perplexed look on your face and you're actin' a might strange this morning."

"Where are Callie and Jacob? I want to see the children."

Frank put his hand on her shoulder. "You don't remember?"

"Remember what?"

"When I took them to my mother's house?"

"Why would you take our children there?"

His eyes widened and a broad smile crossed his face. "Did you say *our* children?"

"Yes, *our* children. I want to see them."

He grabbed her by the shoulders. "Is it really you? Oh Mariah, is it?"

Holding her at arm's length, he searched her eyes. "It is you. I see that familiar sparkle in those beautiful green eyes."

"Oh, Frank," she clung to him, "then it really happened. I didn't dream it?" She leaned back and gazed up at him. "I thought I was crazy. I have so much to tell you. About cars, buildings, swimming pools… I flew in an airplane."

He peppered kisses across her face and eyes. "Well, I don't know what that is, but I have a lot to tell you, too."

* * * *

They sat on the front porch, having coffee, while Mariah shared it all. She told him about all the wonders of the twentieth century, starting with the hospital and ending with her airplane ride. She stared up at the sky. "You should have seen the buildings. They were so tall. And there were horseless carriages called cars, telephones… and machines that washed dishes."

"Telephone, huh? Don't suppose you saw something called a taxi?"

"Yes, taxis... lots of them. And the houses. Oh goodness, Frank, you wouldn't believe the furniture and gadgets."

"Well tell me everything. Taylor raised lots of questions and I think you have all the answers. But first, let me get us some more coffee."

It gave her time to think about the only night she hadn't told Frank about. It served no purpose. Although she and David had shared a bed, nothing had happened except she finally realized the meaning of true love. Not just loving someone, but sharing oneself totally with that special person—putting aside inhibitions and fears. Hearing David talk about his feelings for his wife and the passion they shared, had made her realize how much she missed Frank… showed her the changes she needed to make for him if she ever got the chance. Now the opportunity was here and he was in for a pleasant surprise.

When he came back out, he set their coffee on the table between the wicker chairs and walked to the porch railing. She rose and joined him. The aroma of honeysuckle hung heavy in the air. She placed her hand atop his and gazed across at their old barn. "You know, for as wondrous as it was to experience all those things I told you about, I wouldn't trade my life here for any of it. All I wanted was to come home to you and the children."

He draped an arm over her shoulder and pulled her close. "I never gave up hope, but I have to give Taylor credit. She was determined to find a way back, too. She's a fighter that one. One thing for sure, though, she's not a cook." He gazed into his wife's eyes. "For all Taylor's shortcomings, I'll bet somewhere in 2002, David Morgan is feeling just as happy as I am today."

In Mariah's mind, the thought that Frank had slept with Taylor niggled her, but based on the love shining in his eyes, Mariah knew the answer wasn't important. He loved *her* and that was all that mattered. Taylor was a lifetime away.

Mariah took his hand. "Since the children are gone, why don't we go upstairs and make up for some lost time."

She led him into the house and to the bedroom. The look on his face was worth all the airplane rides in the world. Standing before him, she began unbuttoning his shirt, nipping at his exposed skin. His breath hitched and she took delight in his reaction. She paused for a moment and peered up at him. "It's all so strange. We'll probably never know how it happened or why."

He tumbled her to the bed and nuzzled her neck. "Enough for now, but remind me… next time we hear a thunderstorm brewing, we're headin' for the root cellar."

Mariah chuckled and worked to unbuckle his belt. "I may have never met Taylor, but I sure feel like she's my sister in time. I hope she's doing something equally as fun."

The End

ABOUT THE AUTHOR

Born and raised in California, Ginger and husband Kelly, who happens to be her greatest fan, moved to Tennessee in 2004. Overcoming culture shock took a while, but she continues to write, finding inspiration in the vast number of southern historical areas. She's multi-published in several genres, but her favorite remains historical romance with a western flavor. Besides writing and promoting her work, she always manages to find time to enjoy her grandson, Spencer. The cheerful and patient way he deals with his autistic challenges inspires her to keep doing what she loves—being an author and his Nee Nee!

OTHER BOOKS WE LOVE BOOKS BY GINGER SIMPSON

Ages of Love
Destiny's Bride
First Degree Innocence
Sarah's Passion
Sarah's Heart
Ellie's Legacy
Time Invested
Culture Shock
Embezzled Love
A Novel Murder
Hattie's Heroes
Ginger Simpson Special Edition

BOOKS WE LOVE
http://bookswelove.net
and Books We Love Spice
http://spicewelove.com

Top quality books loved by readers,
Romance, Mystery, Fantasy, Suspense
Vampires, Werewolves, Cops, Lovers.
Young Adult, Historical, Paranormal